Barbara Allen met Michael Townsend in a hospital rehab ward, and there was where her dilemma began.

He'd had surgery on his knee and was assigned to her for rehabilitation. Her job was to get him ready to resume his position in the NBA. His job, it seemed, was to get her in a position in his bed.

Why a young, gorgeous, wealthy man like Michael would be interested in a widow old enough to be his mother—and at least ten pounds overweight—Barbara couldn't fathom. Genetics played a big role in her smooth caramel-brown complexion, but was also responsible for her forty-two-inch hips and forty-C bustline. Maybe that was it, she surmised. Perhaps he had some kinky mother fixation.

Not a chance, according to Michael.

He'd told her on more than one occasion that he thought of her in a lot of ways, but never as his mother....

DONNA HILL

began writing novels in 1990. Since that time, she's had more than forty titles published, which include full-length novels and novellas. Two of her novels and one novella were adapted for television. She has won numerous awards for her body of work. She is also the editor of five novels, two of which were nominated for awards. She easily moves from romance to erotica, horror, comedy and women's fiction. She was the first recipient of the Trailblazer Award and currently teaches writing at the Frederick Douglass Creative Arts Center. Donna lives in Brooklyn with her family. Visit her Web site at www.donnahill.com.

DONNA HILL

Love Becomes Her

This novel is dedicated to my Aunt Marjorie who
instilled in me from the instant I could read the love of
books and writing. Thank you Auntie!

 KIMANI PRESS™

ISBN-13: 978-1-58314-774-0
ISBN-10:   1-58314-774-8

LOVE BECOMES HER

Copyright © 2006 by Donna Hill

www.kimanipress.com

Printed in U.S.A.

Dear Reader,

Thank you so much for choosing *Love Becomes Her*, the first book in the PAUSE FOR MEN series. I do hope you enjoyed meeting Barbara, Stephanie, Ann Marie and Elizabeth and the men who love them. Whoever said that moving past forty was time to turn in your pumps, haven't met "the girlz"!

I had a great time crafting their stories and hopefully bringing you some moments of entertainment and enlightenment. Each of their stories is about taking a stand for yourself and not being afraid when confronted with the obstacles that life throws in your path.

Stay tuned for the next installment, *Saving All My Loving*, which will feature Ann Marie and her dilemma when her estranged husband, Terrance Bishop, wants to come back in her life. There are more twists and turns in store for Barbara, Stephanie and Elizabeth, as well. But, of course, I can't give it away. You'll have to read the book!

Donna Hill

Chapter 1

The winds of change blew a nasty gust of havoc from one end of Morningside Drive to the other. It knocked over unchained garbage cans, rattled windows and stirred up unswept trash. As fate would have it, there were only a selected few whose doors were not only knocked on but kicked in.

Barbara Allen lifted the sheer white curtain from her third-floor bedroom window and peeked outside. The sky was dull gray, the clouds as heavy as a maternity ward of expectant mothers. Stately brownstones were shrouded in fog, reminiscent of a scene out of an old English movie, but the lively radio voices of the KISS FM Wakeup Club playing in the background made the surreal come down to earth.

"Thank God it's Friday." She dropped the curtain back into place before sitting on the side of her bed.

She stuck her feet into her thick-soled white shoes, the third piece of her standard white ensemble. Finding something to wear five days a week hadn't been a problem for close to fifteen years. As a licensed rehabilitation therapist, white was de rigueur.

Barbara enjoyed her work at New York's Cornell University Medical Center. On the orthopedic unit where she worked, she'd met everyone from the grandmother with a hip replacement to the star athlete with a torn tendon.

She picked up her carryall bag from the foot of the bed and walked into her living room en route to the front door, but stopped short. Two empty wineglasses sat in proud accusation on her coffee table. A hot flash from the previous evening played with her mind: a little wine, some easy jazz, a cool breeze and a man young enough to be her son.

The alarm of her cell phone rang on her hip, its gentle vibration sending an unexpected thrill to shimmy down the inside of her thighs. It had been a long time if the vibration from a cell phone could get her going. Maybe she should have let that young boy stay the night. What he may have lacked in experience he could make up for with energy. She chuckled to herself at the ridiculousness of the notion and wondered what the girls would have to say. What she should have done was never let him within ten feet of her apartment in the first place. What had she been thinking? Hmmph, she knew what she'd been thinking. Fortunately, good sense prevailed and not a minute too soon.

Barbara gingerly picked up the glasses with the tips of her fingers as if they had the power to mysteriously conjure Michael up if she stroked them too hard—like a genie in a bottle. Holding them away from her body she went to the kitchen and deposited them in the sink, but not before being pulled into the watery remains that floated in the bottom of the glasses…warm hands, seductive words, sexual starvation…the kiss…almost. *Grrrr.* With a shake of her head she pushed the images aside, slung her bag onto her shoulder and headed out. She was much too old to be longing after that young boy as if he was dessert, she scolded herself while locking the front door. But if just thinking about him felt this good, then… *Barbara, don't let yourself get tripped up in those thoughts. Too long in the unholy state of abstinence must be frying your brain, girl.*

She trotted down the three flights of stairs, her standard shoulder-length ponytail bouncing behind her. She hurried passed the doors of her sleeping neighbors, careful when passing old man Carter's door so as not to stir up that maniac fox terrier of his that thought it was a pit bull. The dog was no bigger than a cat, but noisy enough to wake up the whole building. She chuckled to herself. If she didn't get caught in any unexpected traffic on FDR Drive she should arrive at the hospital in plenty of time to get some coffee and relax before her shift started at eight.

The hospital rehab ward was where she'd met Michael Townsend six months earlier and where her current dilemma began.

He'd had surgery on his knee and was assigned to her for rehabilitation. Her job was to get him ready to resume his position with the NBA. His job, it seemed, was to get her in a position in his bed.

For the life of her, Barbara couldn't fathom why a young, gorgeous, wealthy man would be interested in her: a widow, old enough to be his mother and at least ten pounds overweight. Well…maybe five. Genetics played a big role in her smooth caramel-brown complexion, but was also responsible for her 42-inch hips and 40-C bust line. She was a solid size sixteen, and with her love of a good meal she knew, without careful monitoring, she could shoot past sixteen and keep right on going. Big women ran in her family on both sides like track stars trying to see who gets to the finish line first. Her mother and aunt on her father's side were in a constant dead heat.

Maybe that was it, she'd surmised. She was sure Michael must have some kind of mother-separation issue. But he'd told her on more than one occasion that he may have thought of her in a lot of ways, but mother never entered his mind.

She hadn't said a word to the girls about Michael and it was killing her. She wasn't sure if she'd resisted telling them out of embarrassment or afraid that they would all agree that she should give in and give it up! What would she do then? She knew she couldn't hold out much longer and she needed some advice other than her own.

The wind kicked up a notch as Barbara stepped outside. She hurried toward the corner where her car was parked, just as the first fat drop of rain hit her on the tip of the nose.

April, she thought.

By the time she got her ten-year-old Volvo warmed up enough to drive, rain danced furiously against everything it hit.

"This can't last," she muttered as she watched the wipers wage a fruitless battle against the deluge.

A sudden rapping on her window nearly had her drawing her last breath. She peered through the foggy driver's-side window then pressed the button to lower it.

"Stephanie! Damnit, you nearly scared me to death."

"Open up."

Barbara rolled her eyes and unlocked the doors.

Stephanie jumped in the backseat. "Whew. Almost drowned out there."

"What in the world are you doing going out this early? It's barely 7:00 a.m."

Stephanie laughed in that way of hers that made you believe that life was simply wonderful all the time.

"Going out! Girl, I'm just coming in. Long night."
She laughed again, followed by a delicate yawn.

Barbara shook her head in amazement. Stephanie
Moore was the party girl of the quartet and at least four
nights out of five she could be found in some night-
club or four-star restaurant with any one of an assort-
ment of handsome, eligible and not-so-eligible men.
All work related, she would insist during their weekly
Friday-night soirees. And the remaining trio would
regularly *um-hmmm* her with raised brows of doubt.

Stephanie's job as senior publicist for H. L. Ruben
& Associates, one of the most powerful PR agencies
in the country, was demanding on a variety of levels,
the most demanding of which was keeping the company's high-profile, high-paying clients happy and
scandal free. Suffice it to say, Stephanie was a pro
who could put such a convincing spin on a bad situation that you would walk away believing that the
bad situation was truly a blessing. And she had the
looks to go with the job. She could have easily been
a runway model and had done some print work right
out of college, but felt it was not her true calling. But
she maintained her flair for fashion and her makeup
on clear, cinnamon-toned skin, framed with an expensive "I can't believe it's a weave," complete with
strawberry-blond highlights that were always a
showstopper. Stephanie Moore was a Tyra Banks
look-alike without the big boobs.

"So who was it this time?" She glanced at Stephanie in the rearview mirror and swore she saw a small bruise on the side of Stephanie's neck. It was then that she noticed that Stephanie was actually holding the top of her blouse together. "Steph…is everything okay?" She twisted around in her seat. Stephanie Moore may be a lot of things but disheveled, even at 7:00 a.m., was not one of them.

Stephanie brushed the water from her midthigh black skirt and crossed her long legs. "Yes. Fine. Tired, but fine." She brought her delicate hands toward her neck. "And to answer your other question, just another wannabe. Cute, though. Where are you headed?"

"Work. Where else?"

"Could you drop me off in front of my building? I need to get out of these wet clothes and take a nap. I was dozing in the cab, and the idiot cabdriver let me out too soon."

"Steph, you live three houses down."

"I know, but aren't you going that way?"

Barbara glanced at her friend again in the mirror. Dark circles rimmed the bottom of her lids as if her mascara had entered into the New York Marathon. "You coming over tonight?" she asked, cruising to stop in front of Stephanie's building.

"Wouldn't miss it. What are you fixing?"

"I thought I'd fix my pasta salad. Everyone seems to like it."

"Yum."

"What about you?"

"Wine, of course."

"Of course."

"I caught that note of sarcasm. Can I help it if you, Ann Marie and Ellie are better cooks than I am? No sense in disappointing you guys with my hopeless dishes." She puckered her lips. "That was one of Brian's biggest complaints. I was great in bed, wonderful to look at but I couldn't boil an egg. Go figure." She shrugged in her patent dismissive fashion, but her tone lacked its usual sass. "His loss." She popped the car door open. "Thanks, Barb. See you tonight."

Before Barbara could respond or ask the questions that hovered on the tip of her tongue, Stephanie had darted out of sight and into her building. For a moment she sat there wondering just what kind of night Stephanie had really had. She turned on the radio and slowly drove off.

She often wished she was more like Stephanie; carefree, secure in her sexuality and not caring much what others thought of her and her choices. Unfortunately she was the polar opposite, hence her dilemma about Michael. And maybe it was just as well.

Barbara arrived with only fifteen minutes to spare before she had to clock in. She went directly to the staff lounge hoping against hope that a fresh pot of coffee would be there to welcome her.

No such luck.

Mildly annoyed, she fished around in the cabinet and took out a can of coffee, determined to get one cup down before what she knew would be a long day ahead.

Just as she poured four scoops of coffee into the coffeemaker, her cell phone rang and not the alarm this time. She glanced down at the tiny, sleek gadget on her hip and saw Elizabeth's number on the illuminated face. She smiled, snatched it up and pressed the green telephone icon.

"Ellie, hi, what's up?"

"I'm gonna kill him!" came the ear-piercing voice, followed by the most heart-wrenching sobs Barbara had ever heard.

Barbara jerked back from the phone in alarm. She frowned, lowered her head and her voice. "Ellie, calm down and tell me what's wrong." Elizabeth Lewis was one of the most stable, sensible women that Barbara knew. She was never ruffled or derailed by unforeseen events. Ellie was the one who held Barbara's hand and her head when her husband, Marvin, died. It was Ellie who was the calm during and after the storm, the only one of the quartet who Barbara felt comfortable telling her deepest secrets to...well, except the Michael thing. So, to hear Ellie come unglued truly meant that the stars were misaligned.

"I know you don't mean that, and who are you talking about? It can't be Matt. I—"

"Don't you dare mention that bastard's name!"

So it was Matt. "Okay," she said gingerly. "Why don't you tell me what happened. I'm sure—"

"After twenty-five years, twenty-five fucking years of my life I give to him and he does this to me!"

Her voice had reached operatic octaves and Barbara still had no clue as to what the "nameless bastard" had done. A door slammed in the background, followed by the sound of shattering glass. *This was serious.*

"Ellie, I can't help you if you don't tell me what's going on."

Elizabeth sniffed hard. "I…I have to get ready for my appointment. I'm sorry for calling you like a crazy person," she said, smoothly sliding back into her calm, in-control self. "I'll see you tonight."

The call disconnected, leaving Barbara standing there more confused than when she first heard Ellie's tirade. She slid the phone back into the case on her hip.

"Barb…"

She turned toward the door. It was her assistant, Sheila.

"Your first patient is here."

"Thanks. I'll be right there." She looked at the percolating coffee, down at her cell phone and then the door. "And it's only eight o'clock," she muttered, walking out.

* * *

Fortunately, the rest of her day had been pure routine, Barbara mused as she did a final check of her two-bedroom apartment. The food was on the warming tray in the living room, the salad was freshly tossed and sitting in the fridge. Stephanie was bringing the wine, Ellie was always good for dessert and Ann Marie was the Caribbean-cuisine queen. She was sure to add some island flavor to their evening. Their favorite jazz station played softly in the background and a brand-new deck of playing cards sat ceremoniously in the center of the table.

She placed her hands on her hips—satisfied. They should be arriving shortly, she thought. Ann Marie was usually the first to arrive. She had a real thing about being early and was always willing to lend a hand with any last-minute doings.

As if she'd conjured her up, Ann Marie rang the doorbell.

"It's raining cats and dogs and *daughters*," she said, shaking out her umbrella and dumping it in the wastebasket that Barbara used for such occasions.

She helped Ann Marie out of her trench coat. "And daughters?"

Ann Marie turned toward Barbara, and her younger-than-her-years face pinched into a pained expression.

"Raquel turned up on me doorstep last night,

complete with suitcases and a long story about leaving 'er 'usband."

"What?"

"You 'eard me," she said, sounding more annoyed than concerned about her daughter's current state of marital un-bliss, her Jamaican accent in full force. She marched off into the living room. "I need a drink."

"Help yourself." She followed Ann Marie inside, noting the three-inch heels. Ann Marie was the only woman she knew who wore high heels to the supermarket. Perhaps it had something to do with the fact that in bare feet, Ann Marie was no more than five feet tall.

Ann Marie pulled a bottle of Courvoisier right out of her Gucci bag, took the top off like a pro and poured herself a healthy glass before Barbara could blink. She marched off to the couch and plopped down, then looked up at Barbara.

"Can you believe it? She's moving back in with me for heaven's sake. What me gon' do?"

"What are you going to do? What about Raquel?"

She sucked her teeth and waved her hand. "Raquel will be fine at some point. The question is, will I?" She took a long swallow of her drink that made Barbara wince, then began rambling in that rapid-fire way of hers, with her accent so thick you needed a translator to interpret.

Barbara held up her hands. "Hold it, hold it.

I'm really not understanding a word you're saying, Ann Marie."

Ann Marie paused, dragged in a deep breath and looked up at Barbara with wide, imploring brown eyes set in a rich chocolate–brown face. She ran her hand through her bone-straight midshoulder-length hair. "How in the world am I supposed to get my groove on with my twenty-three-year-old daughter listening to dear old mom knocking boots in the next room? I'm not the church mouse on the block, if you know what I mean."

Barbara let out a bark of nervous laughter. If that was the worst of Ann Marie's problems, she ain't heard nothing yet. Tonight was going to be more than a little interesting.

Chapter 2

Barbara wasn't quite sure what to say to Ann Marie at the moment, while she gulped down her drink and quickly refilled her glass without taking a breath. So Barbara opted not to press the issue. Knowing Ann Marie, she'd spill it all before the night was over.

"I'm going to start putting the stuff out. Ellie and Steph should be here any minute."

"I'll help you." She put the top back on the bottle, shoved it back down inside her purse then pushed herself up from the chair. "Oh lawd." She slapped her palm to her forehead.

"What?"

"Left de damn curry chicken right in de car. Chile got me so upset, can't t'ink straight."

Barbara chuckled as Ann Marie snatched up her umbrella and darted back outside. She took the salad out of the fridge and put it on the counter next to the dressings. She always did a buffet-style dinner, so everyone was on their own to get what they wanted when they wanted it. She took a quick look around. Ice filled the ice bucket, there was a case of Coors Light in the cooler for Stephanie and four bottles of wine to supplement the wine that Stephanie had promised to bring, for everyone else. But apparently Ann Marie had other plans. Hmm. She'd never known Ann Marie to be a hard drinker and certainly not one to actually carry a bottle of liquor stashed in her purse. The sudden arrival of Raquel must have truly rocked unshakable Annie.

Raquel had been out on her own right out of high school, which Barbara personally thought was much too young, but Ann Marie was adamant about Raquel standing on her own two feet and being a woman. "Can't be having no two grown-ass women in one house," Ann Marie had said. "Make for bad business. I'm the only queen in me castle. Ain't sharing no throne."

From the day Raquel moved into a small studio somewhere in Brooklyn, Barbara had seen her maybe five times in all those years. One of which had been at her wedding. She'd been a beautiful bride. It appeared as if her husband, Earl, loved the ground Raquel walked on. What was so odd about that day was that Ann Marie seemed more relieved than anything else, as if now that Raquel was a married woman, whatever semblance of care and responsibility she had for her daughter was no longer anything she had to concern herself with. Ann Marie barely spoke of her, as if she were no more than some distant relative as opposed to her only child.

Sad, Barbara thought. It was the one thing she'd always wanted in her life, a child of her own. Someone to love and nourish and watch grow up and become a wonderful human being. In her case, that was never to be. She knew that if she'd ever had children she would have spoiled them rotten and bragged about them to everyone who would listen. Ann Marie, on the other hand…

The doorbell chimed.

Ann Marie held a large tray in her hands and the mouthwatering aroma seeping out from beneath the foil made Barbara's stomach knot in anticipation. If there was one thing Ann Marie could do and do well, it was cook. The girl put her foot in it every time. And right behind her was Elizabeth.

Elizabeth hurried in with her tray, as well. "Red velvet cake tonight, ladies."

"Oh my. What's the occasion?" Barbara stepped aside to let her friends in. "You only do red velvet for something major." She shut the door and the bell rang again. She snatched it back open.

"Damn, just close the door in my face. I know I only bring wine but I still can beat all y'all in spades."

Barbara laughed. "Sorry, girl, I didn't see you."

"Yeah, yeah." She stepped in and took off her

Burberry trench coat and hung it up on the rack in the hall.

She looks much better than this morning, Barbara quickly observed, shutting the door for the final time. Maybe it was just the rain that had her looking so out of sorts. She went into the living room where Ann Marie and Ellie were already seated around the coffee table, snacking on celery sticks and dip.

"Y'all don't waste any time," Steph said, announcing her arrival, then taking a seat next to Ellie on the couch. She reached for a carrot. "How's everyone doing?" She took a delicate bite and looked from one woman to the next.

Ellie sighed.

Ann Marie sucked her teeth and rolled her eyes.

"Damn, what did I do?" Stephanie asked.

"Nothing," they muttered in unison.

Steph glanced up at Barbara for some kind of hint as to what was going on, but Barbara only shrugged in response. "I'll get the wine."

"Bring plenty," Ellie said.

Ann Marie got up and followed Barbara into the kitchen. She lowered her voice. "Don't say nutin' to dem about Raquel just yet. Okay?"

Barbara looked at her, perplexed. "Fine, but why not?"

"Me really don't wan' talk 'bout it tonight. Still too pissed and upset."

"Annie, it really—"

Ellie walked in. "What's taking so long? And what are you two whispering about?"

"Nutin'." Ann Marie took two bottles of wine and the ice bucket then walked out.

Ellie watched her leave. "What's with her?"

"I wish I knew." She put her hands on her hips. "The question is, what's with you? What was that phone call about this morning? You had me worried."

"I can't talk about it right now." Her eyes suddenly filled and she sniffed loudly. "It's just so fucking awful." Her mouth trembled and she covered it with her hand.

That was the second time in one day that Ellie had cursed. It was something she didn't do and it sounded like a foreign language coming out of her mouth.

"Ell." She put her hand on Elizabeth's shoulder. "What is it, sweetie?"

She just shook her head. Just then, Stephanie burst into the room.

"Ann Marie forgot the Coors. Are they in the freezer? You know I like mine icy cold," Steph chattered, oblivious to the cloud of tension in the room.

Ellie sucked in a breath and darted for the bathroom down the hall.

Steph frowned then put her hands on her hips. "What is wrong with everybody tonight? Feel like I'm at a wake and no one told me."

"Probably the crappy weather."

"I guess." Steph sounded unconvinced. She stepped closer to Barbara. "Listen, about this morning. I'd really appreciate it if you didn't say anything to the girls."

"Wouldn't think of it," Barbara said. *What's one more secret among friends?*

Chapter 3

Ann Marie dealt the first hand of spades while the ladies ate, drank and drank some more. Before the first game was finished, two bottles of wine were empty and Stephanie was on her third bottle of Coors. They were on a roll.

"Somebody up in here is cheatin'," Ellie said, then began to giggle.

"I don't see what's so funny. I'm losing," Stephanie grumbled. "Think I'm being taken advantage of." She turned the empty bottle up to her lips, frowned then looked around for another one. Not finding one, she pushed herself up out of the chair, stumbled once, righted herself and headed for the kitchen. "The rest of the wine out here?" she yelled.

"In the fridge. And bring some more ice," Barbara called out.

Ann Marie got up. "I'll help before her drunk behind breaks something." She zigzagged her way to the kitchen.

Barbara looked across the table at Ellie. They broke out laughing. Just another Friday night with the girls. A time to let their hair down and act the fool without recriminations.

"Good to see you laughing, Ell. You had me worried." She finished the last of her wine.

Suddenly, as if someone had slapped her, Ellie howled in some kind of agony that scared the hell out of Barbara and had Stephanie and Ann Marie falling all over each other to get into the living room.

"What happened?" they screeched. They turned accusing eyes on Barbara, who was stunned into open-mouthed and wide-eyed silence as Ellie bawled and railed like a baby.

Ellie jumped up from the table, nearly falling down in the process. She grabbed the edge of the table to keep from going face-first on the floor.

Barbara hurried to her side. "Ell, calm down. What is it? Tell me, honey." She put her arms around her and led her to the couch.

Stephanie and Ann Marie sat on the floor at Ellie's feet.

"What got you so twisted, chile?" Ann Marie cooed, patting Ellie's knee.

Stephanie patted the other knee. "You can tell us."

Ellie sniffed hard, her body shuddering. "He… he… The bastard!"

"Who? What bastard?" Ann Marie asked.

"Matt!"

"Matthew? Your husband?" Stephanie asked.

Ellie nodded her head hard. "Don't say his name."

The three women looked at each other in confusion.

Barbara sat down next to Elizabeth. "Ell, just tell us what's wrong. Maybe we can help."

"No one can help me. No one." She covered her face with her hands and cried harder.

"Oh, damn, she's drunk," Steph said.

"Oh, shut up. So are you." Ann Marie patted Ellie's knee a little harder.

"I know that." Stephanie said with conviction. "What's your excuse?"

"What!" Ann Marie tried to stand up and couldn't. "You want a fat lip?"

"Who's gonna give it to me, you?" Stephanie started to giggle. "Take off those damn high heels and I'll just step over you and be done with it." She laughed harder.

Barbara cringed. Ann Marie hated nothing more than to be taunted about her height.

Ann Marie snatched off her shoe quicker than a flash of lightning and raised it over her head ready to bean Stephanie. Not before Barbara, seeing disaster unfold, reached out for the shoe before it connected, but instead tumbled in a heap on the floor between the two would-be gladiators.

Seeing Barbara on the floor set them all off into

a fit of near-hysterical laughter, until Ellie's piercing voice broke through the cacophony.

"Have you all lost your mind? Doesn't anyone care about my problem?"

The laughter stopped as abruptly as it started. Three sets of eyes rested on Ellie's tear-streaked face.

"We would, but you won't tell us what it is we're supposed to care about," Stephanie murmured.

Elizabeth looked from one concerned face to the next. She swallowed and wiped her eyes with the back of her hand. "Matthew wants a divorce."

Barbara's mouth opened and all she could say was her dear friend's name.

Ann Marie whispered, "No," then covered her mouth.

"Not you and Matt," Stephanie muttered.

Barbara scrambled up off the floor and sat back next to Ellie. "What happened, Ell?"

Ann Marie sat up. "You bot' seem so happy."

"When did this happen?" Stephanie asked.

"This morning. Over breakfast." She laughed. "Grits, eggs and homemade hash browns just the way he likes them."

Barbara put her arm around Ellie's shoulders and squeezed. "Ell, what did he say?"

Ellie drew in a breath. "He said…he can't live with me anymore. He…doesn't…love me anymore. He's in love with someone else."

"Matt?" Stephanie asked incredulously.

Ellie nodded.

"Who is she? 'Cause it sound to me like she need her arse whipped."

"Ann Marie," Barbara scolded. "That's not going to solve anything."

"Maybe not, but it would make me feel better."

"Yeah, me, too," Stephanie seconded.

"I've met her. Sweet young thing. Not much older than our daughter! Can you believe that? Oh God!" she wailed.

"Oh, girl, it's probably just a fling. A midlife crisis or something. You know how men get. He'll come to his senses," Stephanie offered.

Ellie reached for her purse, tucked near the arm of the couch. She opened it and pulled out a thick set of folded papers. "Does this read like a midlife crisis to you?" She sniffed and shoved the papers toward her friends.

Barbara opened them up. It was a petition for divorce. She passed them to Ann Marie, who then handed them to Steph.

Ann Marie pushed up from the floor, crossed the room to where she'd left her purse on the table and pulled out her bottle of Courvoisier. She put the bottle under her arm and collected their glasses. She handed a glass to each one and began to pour. "We need a real drink after that."

"You ain't lying," Stephanie said.

Barbara took a hearty sip that went straight from the pit of her stomach to her head. This really was serious.

Chapter 4

Silence hung over the quartet for a good five minutes as they worked on digesting the startling information that Elizabeth had shared. The only sounds were the wail of Miles Davis's trumpet on the stereo and the steady beat of rain pounding against the windows.

Finally, Barbara found her voice. "Have you spoken with a lawyer, Ell?"

Elizabeth nodded. "This morning. Right after that bastard left for work." She sniffed.

"What did your lawyer say?" Stephanie asked.

Elizabeth wiped her eyes to make room for more tears. "He said if I wanted to fight it I could and that basically I could get everything since he…he cheated on me!" she wailed. "I can't believe it. I had that little hussy in my house."

"Don't worry about that now," Ann Marie said. "Just take Matt—I mean that bastard's bags and set them on the curb."

"I don't know if I even want to live there...too many memories." She lowered her head.

"But you deserve that house. You put your heart and soul into it all these years. You stayed home so that he could pursue his degrees and his career. You raised your kids there. That's your house," Stephanie insisted.

"She's right, Ell," Barbara said. "And it's worth a fortune. I wouldn't give it up. Let him find someplace else to live."

Elizabeth sighed heavily. "I guess. Besides, where would I go? I certainly can't live with Desiree or Dawne, they have their own lives. *Ohhh,* what am I going to tell my daughters?" She erupted into a new wave of tears and sobbing.

"Your daughters are grown and doing their t'ing. They are mature young women. They will understand. At least you don't have to worry 'bout dem moving back in wit' you like some daughters," Ann Marie said with disgust. "And really upsetting your life."

Stephanie turned to Ann Marie. "Like who? I know Raquel didn't move back home."

Ann Marie sucked her teeth. "Girl show up on me door bag and baggage. What me gon' do?" She sucked her teeth again.

Elizabeth leaned forward, her red-rimmed eyes wide. "Raquel left Earl?"

Ann Marie looked from one to the other. "Yes."

She muttered something that no one could understand. "Grown chile ain't got no business moving in wit' her mudder."

Elizabeth reached for Ann Marie's hand. "Annie, something awful must have happened for her to leave Earl. Did you talk to her?"

"Me too upset to talk." She shook her head.

"But don't you even want to know what happened?" Stephanie asked, perplexed.

"What can me do even if she tol' me? Nutin'. What me gon' tell Phil when he come back next week?"

"Phil!" the trio sang in unison.

"Girl, you have got to be kidding," Stephanie croaked.

"He's fine and everything, but that's your child. What are you worried about him for?" Elizabeth asked.

"I have a one-bedroom apartment for a reason. Don't keep no company that's not sharing me bedroom, if you get what I mean."

"But that's your daughter, Ann Marie," Barbara scolded, unable to fully understand Ann Marie's total lack of concern for her child. It was unreasonable and cruel, not characteristics that she associated with Ann Marie. But when you put folk's backs up against the wall there was no telling if they were going to come out swinging or singing. She always felt that Ann Marie's relationship with her daughter was not all that it could be, but this turned her stomach. There had to be more to it than what Ann Marie was saying.

"Yes, she's my daughter wit' a 'usband." She pushed herself up from the floor and fixed herself another drink. "I don't want to talk 'bout it no more." She took a long swallow and for an instant her gaze connected with Barbara's, and Barbara was stunned to see fear in Ann Marie's eyes.

"You know what's best for you and your daughter," Barbara said, letting Ann Marie off the hook. "But don't let a man come between you and your child. That's all I'm gonna say besides pass me the bottle. I really need a drink now."

The women giggled, releasing some of the tension in the room as Ann Marie refilled everyone's glass. They sipped in silence.

"What would you do if you didn't want to have sex anymore, but the person you didn't want to have sex with was your boss?"

The silence was officially broken.

Chapter 5

All eyes turned in Stephanie's direction. She had a pinched look on her face, as if she'd swallowed something sour, but the look of defiance that generally hovered in her caramel-colored eyes was missing. Barbara immediately thought of the episode that morning and knew her gut feelings about Stephanie had some merit. This she had to hear.

Ann Marie was the first to speak up. "What you say, girl? Your boss? You been doing the do with your boss?"

"Ann!" Barbara admonished. She lowered her voice. "Is it true? You and Conrad what'shisname?"

Stephanie bobbed her head and took a sip of her drink.

"Well, I'll be," Elizabeth murmured, forgetting her own drama. "How long?"

"About a year."

"And you're just telling us," they cried off-key.

"It wasn't supposed to be anything, you know. Just a few dates."

"Is that how you got your last promotion?" Ann Marie asked.

Stephanie looked at her and rolled her eyes. "I was going to get the promotion, anyway."

The trio *um-hmmmed* her.

"Fine." She jumped up. "I knew I shouldn't have said anything. I'm not an idiot. I didn't get to where I am on my back. I work hard for everything I have in the boardroom or the bedroom," she slurred. "I thought you all were my friends."

"Damn, she actually looks like she's gonna cry," Ann Marie muttered in awe, the four glasses of alcohol making Stephanie look like one of those desert mirages floating in front of her. "Sit down. You're making me dizzy."

"Yes, please," Elizabeth said, rubbing her eyes. "You're giving me an ache or something."

Barbara sputtered a giggle. "Oh, what a night," she sang badly and raised her glass in a toast. "To Ellie, who after twenty-five years of marriage is being kicked to the curb by her philandering husband and a hussy."

"Hear, hear!"

"To Ann Marie, who can't get it on anymore, with her daughter in the next room, and is now afraid her stuff will dry up and be no more good!"

Even Ann Marie fell out laughing.

"A toast to Stephanie, who's been secretly canoodling with her boss and can't figure out how to say, 'Boss, I ain't feeling this no more…but can I still get my raise?'"

Fits of laughter filled the room.

"And to dear old Barbara Allen, who is being pursued by a man young enough to be her son."

This time even the stereo and the wind outside went silent.

"Stop playing, Barbara," Elizabeth said. "You would be the last person in the world to fool around, especially with a man young enough to be your son."

"Yeah. Give me that glass. You've had too much to drink." Stephanie reached for the glass, but Barbara snatched it away.

"We all have," Ann Marie muttered.

"Why is it so hard to believe that someone would be interested in me?" Barbara shouted, then struggled to her feet. She weaved back and forth for a moment and all eyes followed her swaying motion until she steadied herself. "I'm attractive."

"Yes, you are," they agreed.

"I'm still sexy."

"*Um-hmmm.*"

"A lot of men would want me."

"Of course," Elizabeth said.

"Well, did you do it or didn't you?" Stephanie asked, getting straight to the point.

"Scared."

"Of what?" Ann Marie asked.

Barbara plopped down on the love seat and stretched her legs out in front of her. "I haven't been with a man since Marvin died."

"Ohhh," they chorused in sympathy.

"Well, it's like riding a bike. Once you get on, it all comes back to you," Ann Marie said.

"That's very true," Stephanie added.

Elizabeth sniffed. "I wouldn't know. That bastard was the only man I've ever been with."

"Ohhh," they chimed.

"I don't know if I should get involved...like that," Barbara said. "He's a patient of mine."

"It's not the same thing as *doctor*–patient," Ann Marie offered.

"That's true," Stephanie concurred.

"How do you feel about him?" Elizabeth asked.

Barbara turned gentle eyes on her friend. "I like him...a lot."

"So go for it, girl. You only live once. It's not like you're going to marry him," Stephanie said.

"And every healthy able-bodied woman needs some young lovin' every now and then," Ann Marie added.

The trio nodded in agreement.

Barbara sighed. "Wouldn't it be ideal if women could just sit back and pick who they wanted, when they wanted, how they wanted, with no recriminations."

"Yep! Old, young, very young, married, single, rich, poor, your employee or your boss," Stephanie said.

"Yeah, and they'd all been previously screened," Elizabeth said. "And you could find them all in one place."

"Yeah, like a male supermarket!" Ann Marie joked.

"Or like in a department-store window," said Stephanie. "You could window-shop for a man. And they would have to be returnable."

Barbara giggled. "Yes, they'd all be posing in the window, like puppies in a pet shop. Pick me, pick me." She giggled again. "And the women would pause to take a look at the men and move along to the next window."

"*Um-hmmm.*"

"Wish there was a place like that," Elizabeth said wistfully.

"Shopping for men would certainly keep our minds off of our own troubles," Ann Marie said.

"But sometimes you just want to look, you know," Barbara said.

"And if women sat around ogling men all the time…well, you know what they are called," Stephanie said before finishing off her drink.

"Still, it would be nice if there was a place where you go to look and fantasize and maybe—" Barbara shrugged "—who knows, maybe something would happen if you wanted it to."

"*Um-hmmm.*"

They looked at each other, and their faith, love and

trust in their friendship stripped away any inhibitions they may have had and they began talking all at once.

They talked and ate and drank until the sun beamed through the windows of Barbara's apartment. And they'd come up with an idea that was so far-fetched and deliciously exciting that it simply had to work.

Chapter 6

The aroma of frying bacon tickled Ann Marie's nose. She turned on her side and tried to ignore it. She needed sleep, more sleep. She put the pillow over her head hoping that it would block out the *tap, tap, tapping* in her skull. She pulled her knees up to her chin. That didn't help, either, and if she didn't know better she'd swear someone was calling "Mama."

Mama! Damn. She sat straight up in bed, the covers falling off her nude body, and her head did a three-sixty. She pressed her palms to her temples, hoping to slow down the spinning.

"Yes," she croaked. Her tongue felt like a glue strip.

Her bedroom door eased open. Ann Marie pulled the sheet up to her chin.

"I fixed breakfast," Raquel said. "I thought you might be hungry."

"Thanks. You didn't have to do that."

"It's okay. I wanted to." She stepped into the room, balancing the tray.

Ann Marie looked at her daughter and saw the spitting image of the child's father; the dark, almost haunting eyes, shadowed by sweeping black brows and a mass of hair that resembled black cotton candy. Oh, yes, Terrance was a looker and so was his daughter.

Raquel gently placed the tray on her mother's lap. "I'll leave you to your food." She turned to go.

Was that a motherly pang she felt tightening her chest at the sad look in her daughter's eyes? She felt as if she should say something, do something. But she had no idea what.

The door closed quietly behind Raquel. The moment was gone.

Ann Marie toyed with her bacon and eggs. She took a sip of orange juice. What was she going to do about Raquel? There was no way she could let her stay indefinitely. Her mama had put her out on her own at sixteen and she'd never looked back, although she'd wanted to. But her mama had been very clear about having another grown woman in the house beside her. No good, her mama said.

Her situation was different, however. There was more to it than simply having another woman in the house, even if it was her daughter. She sighed and took a bite of bacon. She couldn't explain it to the girls and she never even voiced her fears out loud. The truth—she was afraid. She couldn't face the look of disappointment that she knew would linger in those beautiful eyes. So instead of risking that, she would have to make Raquel go, go to wherever it was she needed to be. Anyplace other than here.

By the time Ann Marie finished her breakfast, bathed and dressed, Raquel was gone.

Ann Marie moved slowly through her one-bedroom condo. She checked the living room where Raquel spent the night. Everything was in its place. The smoked-glass tables were spotless, the pillows on the couch were properly fluffed, no dust on the wood floors, and her imported area rug was exactly where it was supposed to be. The bathroom and kitchen were equally as spotless. It was almost as if no one lived there. Almost.

She breathed in deeply the empty air, hoping perhaps to catch at least a brief hint of Raquel's scent. Even that was absent.

She should be relieved. She put her breakfast dishes in the dishwasher. Oddly, she wasn't. Walking into the bathroom, she opened the medicine cabinet in search of her bottle of Extra Strength Tylenol. She shook out two gel caps and tossed them down her throat with some water. It would take a good ten to twenty minutes for the full effect to kick in. They'd really tied one on last night and she was paying dearly for it this morning.

Ann Marie frowned, trying to bring the events of

the prior evening into focus as she walked back to her bedroom. It seemed that everyone was in some kind of turmoil, as if a cloud of unrest had settled on their quiet block. Ellie with her cheating husband; Stephanie with a boss who wanted more than nine-to-five and good old conservative Barbara being pursued by a boy toy.

She shook her head and laughed. Then snippets of their conversation began to come back to her, something about showcasing men.

Right! She snapped her fingers as the details became clear. A slow smile tipped the corners of her mouth. Yes, even in the light of day their idea was a winner. And if memory served her, she was the first link in the chain.

Picking up her pace, she went into the kitchen and put on a pot of coffee. She'd need to be clearheaded.

While the coffee brewed, Ann Marie turned on her computer in the small room at the end of the hall that she used as an office. She placed her notebook and several empty manila folders on the desk then turned on the printer. To keep her company she popped in a John Legend CD then went to get her coffee.

If there was one thing Ann Marie knew hands down it was a good piece of property—and a man, of course. But finding a true gem of a building and understanding its potential gave her a rush equivalent to sexual expectation.

She smiled to herself as she added Sweet'n Low to her coffee with a dash of canned milk.

Ann Marie had been in the real-estate game for more than fifteen years. Her master's degree in urban economics helped her to fully appreciate the power of ownership and how easily poor communities can become no more than a memory in a matter of a few short years once an investor with a keen eye discovers the value of a particular area.

She'd been telling her friends for years that they needed to invest in some property. Of course, Ellie was already married with a home, but Barbara and Stephanie came up with one excuse after another why they couldn't buy.

The area of Harlem where they lived, an area where houses couldn't be given away ten years earlier, was now so expensive that it was unreachable for most. At least she owned her apartment, and a four-story apartment building on the lower east side of Manhattan that was finally paying for itself after eight years. And she had a town house.

Yes, she'd done well for herself without the help or support of anyone. Her mother putting her out and her leaving Terrance were the best things to happen to her. Yes, they were.

Her throat tightened. No, she didn't need anyone. And the quicker Raquel understood that the better off she would be.

She took her coffee cup into her office. She had work to do and wanted to have some viable locations to show the girls as soon as possible.

Just as she sat down in front of the computer screen, the phone rang. She let it ring three times while she debated whether or not to pick it up. Curiosity won out.

She picked up the extension off the wall in the office.

"Hello?"

"Hey, baby."

"Phil." A fire lit her up inside at the sound of his voice. "Where are you?"

"Still out in L.A. I was hoping to leave on Monday, but things are taking longer than we anticipated."

"Oh." She sat down in the leather swivel chair and slowly spun in a circle, cradling the phone to her ear.

"Don't sound so down, baby. I should be home by next weekend. And then we can spend five whole days making up for lost time."

She laughed then stopped suddenly. *Raquel.*

"You, okay? Something wrong?"

"No, I'm fine," she lied. "Just missing my man, that's all." At least that part was true.

"Next time I'll arrange for you to go with me."

"I should have come this time. You know how much I love California."

"I know. But this trip was real work. The director and executive producer have been bumping heads since we got here. The E.P. swears there's not enough money in the budget for the scenes that the director wants to shoot. So we've been scouting out new locations. I think everyone is finally satisfied. I'm pretty hopeful that these scenes won't take more than a couple of days."

Good, by that time Raquel would be out of the house.

"So what have you been up to?"

"Hmm, just an evening with the girls last night."

Phil chuckled. "I would love to be a fly on the wall at one of those gatherings."

"I bet you would."

"So, what was it this time?"

She often came back from the girls' night out and told Phil about some of the things they talked about: finances, the state of the world, vacations, job woes and men, of course. But this time was different. They'd all shown a side of themselves that they'd never revealed before—a totally vulnerable side, a side of hurt and uncertainty. They'd entrusted each other with secrets, and this time those secrets were sacred.

"Hmm, nothing special, just the usual stuff."

"Okay, well, listen, I have to run. Need to be on the set in twenty minutes. Behave until I see you."

Ann Marie giggled. "What fun would that be?"

Phil laughed in return. "Talk to you soon."

"Bye."

Slowly she hung up the phone. In the year and a half that she'd been with Phil she'd never outright lied to him. What had that storm blown in yesterday?

Chapter 7

Elizabeth sat in the solitude of her ultramodern kitchen. The black-and-white space was equipped with every tool to make even the most resistant cook want to try their hand at being a chef. Cooking was Elizabeth's passion. She so enjoyed the looks of delight on her family and friends' faces when she'd present them with a new creation.

She'd transferred her culinary love to her twin daughters, Dawne and Desiree, who ran a small health-food café and grill in the West Village. They did all of the cooking themselves and enjoyed it, and from the booming business they did, so did their customers.

Elizabeth looked around. Her entire home was a showplace. She took pride in creating a special feel and tone to the four-bedroom brownstone. She'd spend hours scouring catalogs or hunting through out-of-the-way shops for the perfect pillow, throw rug, handmade sculpture, quilt or piece of art. Her family and her home were all she had. It was who she was.

Her throat muscles clenched as a single tear slid down her cheek. She thought she had no more tears to shed. Her eyes were swollen and her throat was raw.

Matthew hadn't even bothered to come home last night, and if he did, she'd been too drunk to notice, and he was long gone by the time she woke up. Just as well.

What was she going to tell her daughters, that she was a failure, another woman who couldn't hold on to her husband?

Damn you, Matthew! She hurled a mug across the room. The sound of it crashing against the opaque-colored stucco wall was equal to a sonic boom inside her head. She covered her face with her hands and wept.

The ringing front doorbell penetrated her sobs. Through bleary eyes she looked up, confused. It rang again. Her head pounded. She pushed herself up from the chair and went to the front door. It was probably the UPS delivery she was expecting.

"Just leave it," she croaked through the door. She'd hate for Jeff, her regular delivery guy, to see her in such a mess. The thought of how bad she must look sent her off on another crying jag.

"Ellie, it's me, Barbara. Open the door."

"Go away, Barbara."

"Elizabeth, if you don't open this door, I'm going to call the police and tell them I smell gas. You know I will." She waited, determined.

If there was one thing everyone knew about Barbara Allen it was that she was good at her word. The last thing she needed today was to have the police breaking down her door. Elizabeth wiped her runny nose on the sleeve of her robe then reluctantly unlocked the door.

Barbara stopped in shock at the disheveled look of Elizabeth. "What in the devil happened to you?"

Elizabeth ignored the question, turned and walked back into the kitchen. Barbara closed and locked the door then followed Elizabeth inside.

"Ell, what's going on? You look awful." She put her purse on the kitchen table. "Did something else happen with…you know who?" She was still mindful of not mentioning the unmentionable one's name.

Ellie shook her head, her wild and matted hair swinging around her face like an old beat-up mop. "Isn't being served with divorce papers after twenty-five years enough?" she snapped.

Barbara took the verbal assault in stride. She sat down and waited for Elizabeth to talk. She'd sit there with her friend all day if need be. She reached across the table and took Elizabeth's hands in her own.

"Ell," she said gently, "I know it doesn't seem like it, but it will be all right. It's going to hurt like hell, but you will get through it."

Elizabeth looked at Barbara through swollen, red eyes. "How, Barb? How am I going to make it without him? He and the girls are my whole life. The girls are out on their own." She slowly shook her head, still in disbelief. "I...thought that now it would be time for me and Matt. Do all the things we didn't get a chance to do." Her voice cracked, the pain so intense that it hurt Barbara's heart. She could kill Matt with her bare hands for doing this to Ellie. She held Elizabeth's hand tighter, letting her get it all out.

"I've never been anything but a wife and mother." She blinked hard and lost fighting back the tears. "What am I going to do? I've never even had to work since college. Matthew took care of me. Oh, God." She covered her face and broke down, her shoulders shuddering and shaking with the force of her sobs.

Barbara came around the table, dragging her chair with her. She snatched Elizabeth's hands away from her face and stared into her eyes.

"Now, you listen to me. Snap the hell out of it. If Matthew doesn't have the good sense God gave him, then you are better off without him. Period. No, you didn't deserve to be hurt like this, but it happened. Happens every damn day of the week and it'll keep happening. Now is not the time to feel sorry for yourself. If you do then he's won, plain and simple."

"But—"

Barbara held up her hand. "No buts. This is an ugly blessing in disguise. A time for you to take charge of your own life for a change instead of being the extension of everyone else's."

"You don't understand, I—"

"Yes, I do understand. You're hurt and scared and angry. But you can't let those emotions paralyze you into inaction."

Elizabeth started to protest.

Barbara stood and pulled Elizabeth to her feet. "First things first. Take a shower, comb your hair, put on some makeup and get dressed. We have work to do."

Chapter 8

Barbara hadn't felt this good about something in a very long time, she thought as she waited for Elizabeth to return. She felt energized and it was just the thing to get each of them out of the slump they'd fallen into. They'd be so busy they wouldn't have the time to dwell on what ailed them. And it would give her the time and space she needed to think clearly about her and Michael and the invisible line they'd crossed.

Michael had called earlier in the day. He'd wanted to see her. Against her better judgment she'd told him he could stop by for a little while and she'd prepare brunch.

When she opened the door for him and saw him smile at her as if he'd gotten the greatest gift of his life, she kicked her inhibitions to the side. If only for one night, as dearly departed Luther would say. But in her case, if only for one afternoon.

"Come on in. I was just finishing up in the kitchen.

Have a seat in the living room and make yourself comfortable." How she was able to speak as calmly as she did was a mystery to her, especially with her heart pounding at an alarming rate, her stomach in an uproar and her knees about as weak as a newborn's.

"Let me help. After all, I did kind of bully my way over here." He chuckled. "It's the least I can do."

She shrugged. "Sure. Come on."

He followed her into the kitchen. "Wow, what a spread."

She'd prepared honey wings, grilled chicken strips, a tossed salad, yellow rice and peas, codfish patties and a side of potato salad.

She offered up a nervous grin. "I wasn't sure what you liked." She twisted her hands together.

"Well, if you wanted to impress me with your cooking skills, it's a wrap." He walked over to the counter where the food was laid out. "Definitely impressive and it smells delicious." He turned to her. "Thanks." He ran his tongue across his lips, slid his hands into his jeans pocket and leaned against the fridge.

She nodded, sure that if she spoke, her voice would be a squeaky version of Minnie Mouse.

His body took up so much space, she observed absently. At six foot six, two hundred and sixty pounds of sinewy muscle covered in toffee-toned skin, he was all man, even as the slight gleam in his dark eyes and the curve of his wide mouth evoked images of the mischievous boy he once was.

"You want to stay in here or move to the dining room?" he asked with a toss of his head over his shoulder toward the adjoining room.

Barbara swallowed over the dryness in her throat, snapping back from her evaluation. The living room was a little too close to her bedroom. "Um, in here is fine. Then we don't have to shuffle everything around."

"Great. So, what can I help you with? Point me in the right direction."

"The, uh, dishes and glasses are in the cabinet behind you."

Michael took out plates and glasses and set them on the table near the window in the eat-in kitchen.

Barbara fumbled in the silverware drawer and dropped several forks and knives before finally getting it together.

"There's a pitcher of iced tea in the refrigerator, unless you want something else," she said, setting the silverware on the table.

"Iced tea is fine."

"I usually do things buffet style, so help yourself to whatever and how much you want."

Michael loaded his plate with some of everything and ate heartily. Barbara, on the other hand, was playing a game of chess with her food, strategically moving it around on the plate from one position to another.

Michael held his glass of iced tea to his lips. "Not hungry?" His brow rose with his question.

"Guess my eyes were bigger than my stomach." She started to reach for her glass but changed her mind midway, certain that with her hands going through a bout of nervous palsy, the liquid would slosh all over her yellow linen tablecloth.

"I really like your hair out," he said.

She patted her hair while looking away. She'd spent forty-five minutes in the mirror with her electric curling iron, trying to put a little bounce in her usual straight, pulled-back style. It must have paid off.

"Thanks."

"I hope it was for my benefit." He slowly put down his glass and folded his hands on the table.

"Oh, this. I...wanted to do something different. The other look thing is for work," she babbled. Geez, where had her conversation skills run off to? They must have ducked under the table, where she wanted to go at the moment.

"I like it. You should wear your hair that way more often." He took his napkin and wiped his mouth. "The food was delicious. This could become addictive." He smiled slowly. "If you let it."

Barbara didn't know where to look, so she stared at her full plate.

"Maybe next time I can do the honors."

Her gaze shot in his direction. *Next time!*

"I fix a mean pot of chili." He winked.

Chili gave her gas. That would be her way out. "Good to know." She stood abruptly. "Let me clean up the table." She reached for his plate. He grabbed her hand. She stopped breathing. *Damn, he was fine*.

"When are you going to stop running from me?"

"I'm…running. I mean, *not* running."

"Of course you are." He held on to her hand as he came around the table and stood in front of her. "I swear I won't hurt you. Just give me a chance. That's all I ask, Barbara, a chance to make you happy."

"Michael." Her expression was one filled with doubt. "We come from two different worlds. And—"

"That's what will make it all the more explosive when those two worlds collide."

Before she could protest further, he kissed her. Kissed her the way she'd read about, seen on the big screen and daytime soap operas. Kissed her with a tender passion that dampened her panties and had her good sense taking a leave of absence.

She gave in. Gave in to the kiss and gave of herself. She could feel all the knots of doubt begin to loosen as he held her close, his long, hard fingers playing a concerto up and down her spine. She gave in to his warmth, letting it seep into all the places inside her that had been cold for far too long. She gave in to the feel of his erection that pushed with urgency against her pelvis, and she pushed back in the way that she remembered, that sensual before-sex dance that forced you to toss caution to the wind.

His lips moved back from hers and he looked into her eyes.

"I won't lie to you. I want you. Bad. I can't break it down any simpler than that. But I want you to feel the same way." He waited a beat. "Do you?"

"Yes," she said, surprised and relieved by her own admission. She took his hand. "Come on. If we stay in here, we might hurt ourselves with the knives and forks on the table."

Barbara felt the heat of his body as he walked behind her. She was shaking so badly she was certain she would crumble in a heap and this fantasy would come to a grinding halt.

She stopped in front of the door, hesitated for a moment. *There's still time to change your mind,* an inner voice whispered.

Michael's lips brushed the side of her neck. She moaned and grabbed the doorknob for support. Some outside force must have turned the knob because she was frozen in place. The door opened and they stepped inside.

It was like a dream the way he undressed her, piece by piece, tossing each item on the chaise longue.

Barbara wished it was dark in her bedroom. Dim enough to hide her body's imperfections from his exploring eyes.

As she stood before him, she saw the no longer perky breasts, airtight-stomach and track runner thighs. Instead, she saw the body of a forty-nine-year old woman who had lived life, and life, as it was wont to do, took its toll.

She didn't want to believe him when he said that she was exquisite, a woman in every sense of the word. It couldn't be true, her mind said, even as the tenderness of his touch worked to shatter her misconceptions.

"Let me look at all of you."

No! her body screamed, but she couldn't move, couldn't run and hide while his gaze held her in place.

Barbara felt like tender meat on the holiday grill, his eyes the hot coals that cooked her from the inside out until she was ready to be devoured by the hunger that his expression cried for.

She *would* think about food at a time like this, and giggled nervously at the image dancing in her head.

Michael reached out and touched her right breast and she felt faint. Her eyes drifted shut for an instant then shot open when his fingers began to play with her clit.

Oh…my…God. He's not going to do that, is he? Oh…yes…he…is!

He was on his knees and his mouth replaced his fingers.

Barbara's inner thighs trembled and even her firm

behind vibrated. She grabbed his shoulders in a death grip to keep from falling on the floor.

Michael languidly rose, nipping her skin as he did.

Somehow Barbara found herself supine on her bed with every nerve ending jumping for joy.

When Michael entered that dark space that had been empty for so long she wanted to shout hallelujah. Instead, she cried out, "Michael."

Barbara lay curled next to the warmth of Michael's body. The wonder of what had transpired between them had her thoughts and head swimming upstream. Ann Marie was right. It was like riding a bike. She hadn't forgotten a thing and learned some new tricks along the way. And when Michael told her again that she was beautiful—she felt it and she believed.

She'd wanted to spend the rest of the day jumping for joy, spinning around naked in her room, reveling in her newfound sexuality. But the practicality of life took root. She'd just made love to a man-child. It felt damn good, there was no doubt about it, and she wanted more and more. That was her fear. So when Michael asked to stay with her for the rest of the day and night, she said no. And then told him on his way out the line that most men give women, "I'll call you."

So here she was, still tingling from the afterglow, sitting in her best girlfriend's house, whose life was in a shambles and she didn't have the heart to spill her own tale all over Elizabeth's perfectly polished kitchen table.

Chapter 9

Stephanie listened to the phone ring and checked the number on the caller ID. *Conrad.* Her heart began to race.

Things had gone too far. Conrad was out of control. She pressed her fist to her mouth as she listened to his voice on the answering machine.

"Steph, if you're there pick up. We need to talk. Stephanie, pick up. I know you're home. Your car is parked out front."

She ran to the window and peeked out from between the slats in the blinds five stories below. Conrad's silver Lexus was in front of her door.

"Open the door or I'm using my key."

She squeezed her eyes shut. In a stupid moment of lust she'd given him her spare key so that he could "slip between her and her sheets whenever he wanted." She would have to get the locks changed and pronto.

She finger fluffed her short do, smoothed her

lemon yellow fitted sweater top over her tight jeans and picked up the phone. "I'm here," she murmured and felt ill.

"I'll be right up."

Stephanie sat in the armchair facing the door as she heard the locks release and watched the knob turn. She slid her hand down between the cushion and felt the security of cold metal brush her fingers. She'd shoot him if she had to. Simple as that.

Conrad walked in, all smiles, and when she looked at him, for a moment she forgot everything she'd promised herself to remember; that he was using her, that he'd physically hurt her, that he was never going to leave his wife and that she wasn't getting any more promotions if she wasn't putting out any more of her body. He'd made that clear the other night.

Instead, she thought about how he made her feel, how he'd awakened the dormant sexuality in her that had spun out of control, how he'd been the first man in her life to help her experience a real orgasm. That had never happened to her before, until she'd met Conrad. He made her do things that she'd only imagined, and she enjoyed it. And he'd become more demanding as the months progressed. As much as he'd begun to disgust her, he still thrilled her, and that was worse than anything else.

"Hey, baby." He crossed the room, leaned down and kissed her long and slow.

"Hi," she whispered when he stepped back.

He looked down at her. "You look tired. Long night?"

That tone was in his voice, the cajoling, demanding tone that preceded the innuendos and accusations.

"Not really." She shrugged. "Just an evening with the girls."

"Hmm." He took his jacket off and tossed it on the couch. "The girls, huh? You sure about that?" His dark eyes grew hard, the line between his brow deepened.

Her breath tightened in her chest. "Of course I'm sure." She stood. He pushed her back down in the chair then leaned over her, locking her in place with his hands on either side of the chair's arms.

"Sure there were no guys there?"

"No," she croaked.

"I don't believe you." He pulled her up by the wrist and up to his chest. His arm wrapped around her body. He pressed his lips to her neck and inhaled her scent. "Show me what you did," he said in an urgent whisper.

"I...didn't do anything."

"I don't believe you." He bit down on her neck and sucked it gently, then with more urgency. "Show me." His free hand slid up her sweater. She trembled at his touch.

"Conrad...please..."

"Yes, I know, baby..."

He lowered her to the floor and as much as she hated what he was doing to her body, she couldn't find the will to resist. Her cries were as much in ecstasy as they were ones for help.

Conrad looked down at her huddled on the floor as he zipped his pants. He smiled as if he truly cared about her. "We have a major new client coming in on Monday. I want you to run the program. You're the best, and if anyone can land this big fish you can."

She turned her head away and tried to cover her shame with her discarded sweater, even as her body still throbbed with pleasure.

"And I promise you, Steph, if you get the account, your bonus will be your biggest ever." He knelt down beside her and with a tenderness that made her heart constrict, he stroked her cheek. "You're so beautiful, you know that." His eyes ran over her face. He took his fingertip, placed it beneath her chin and turned her to face him. "Beautiful," he said again. "And talented…on many levels. That's why I love you, why I want you at my side." He lowered his head and kissed her, then abruptly stood.

"I have to go. Son has a basketball game this afternoon." He adjusted his clothes then picked up his jacket from the couch. "I'll probably be back tonight. Late. Wait up for me."

She nodded. He turned to leave. If she could find the strength, she could reach into the chair cushion, take out the gun and shoot him where he stood. Then it would be over. Finally.

The door closed behind him and he was gone.

The sun was beginning to set when Stephanie came to herself and looked around. She'd stayed there curled in a knot on the floor like discarded laundry for hours. She'd lost track of time. Willing herself to move, she pushed up on her hands and knees and slowly stood.

She glanced down at her nude body, the angry red bruises on her stomach and stickiness between her thighs quick and painful reminders. She shivered and not from a chill. She reached for her clothes on the floor, nearly falling over as her head spun. Holding on to the furniture and the walls, she finally made it to the bathroom. She sat down on the lid of the commode and turned on the tub. At least the hot water would wash away the remnants from the outside, but she didn't think anything could cleanse her battered spirit.

How could she have allowed her life to get so ugly, so out of control? She didn't know what to do, how to fix it. Too many people relied on her and she couldn't let them down. There was no way out. If she quit, she knew that Conrad would blacklist her. She'd never be able to work in New York or any other major city again. If she went to the board, no one would believe her, not to mention how humiliated she would feel, having to confess the extent to which she'd participated over the past year.

She was trapped. Trapped by need, trapped by responsibility and trapped by her body. Conrad knew it and pushed all her hot buttons.

But it had gone too far now and she was afraid. She needed a way out, but she didn't see any open doors in her future.

Her phone rang in the distance. She didn't have the energy or the desire to get up and get it. She turned off the water to listen to the voice coming through the answering machine.

"Steph, it's us, me Barbara and us," she giggled, obviously excited. "We're waiting for you at my house. Hurry up. And bring your laptop."

Stephanie frowned in concentration. Waiting for her? What the hell for? Slowly the pieces began to fall into place and a glimmer of hope settled in her gut. Maybe a door was opening after all.

Chapter 10

When the doorbell rang at about eight o'clock, it was Stephanie who was the last to arrive, looking a bit frayed around the edges. Barbara kept her comments to herself as she quickly ushered Stephanie inside.

"You all right, girl?" she whispered.

"Yeah." She forced a smile that didn't meet her eyes. "Hangover. I was, uh, still asleep when you called."

She put her arm around Stephanie's shoulders. "Not a problem. We were just running our mouths as usual."

Barbara looked especially radiant, as if she'd found the secret of the universe and didn't want to share, Stephanie observed, but she didn't have the energy or her usual level of curiosity to press for details. Maybe it was the hair. It was out and curled instead of tied in that ponytail she usually wore. Yeah, maybe that was it, a new hairdo.

"Everybody here?"

"All in the living room. Ann has some exciting

news. Come on. Stephanie's here," Barbara announced as if they couldn't see that for themselves.

"What happened to you?" Ann Marie blurted out. "You look awful."

"Thanks," Stephanie murmured and rolled her eyes. Ann Marie was always the one looking for a dig, but Stephanie was determined not to let her prying eyes or fast tongue get under her skin tonight. She took a seat at the end of the couch and put her laptop on the table. "So what's with the big pow-wow? She leaned back against the cushions, looking from one to the other.

Ann Marie spoke up, using her polished British accent that she employed when dealing with her realty clients. "After our discussion last night, I did some research on available property in the neighborhood and found three buildings that could meet our needs." She pulled out three printouts from her leather portfolio and placed them on the table. "This one—" she pointed to the first picture "—is on One Hundred and Twenty-seventh Street. This one," she indicated the next picture, "is on One Sixteen. But this one I think is the best." She passed the picture around. "It's a four-story brownstone just off Fifth Avenue on One Twenty-four. It has all the original details, a finished basement, an ample backyard, four bedrooms, two huge sitting rooms and an enormous kitchen. But the best news is that it is in foreclosure, which is good for us."

"What's the bad news?" Barbara asked, ever practical.

"Well," Ann Marie dragged out. "It's in major disrepair. There has been a lot of water damage, the electrical system must be upgraded and it needs a new roof."

The trio's hopeful expressions sank. "Oh," they chorused.

"But there are tons of programs to help buyers with those kinds of repairs," she added quickly to quell their fears. "The thing now is to get in there, make a bid and get the property. The rest will take care of itself. And because it needs so much work, the asking price is much lower than the other two."

"How much are we talking about?" Elizabeth asked.

Ann Marie's lips pinched for a moment, this was always the time when her clients balked. "The asking price is only five hundred and sixty-five thousand."

"Only!" Stephanie squeaked.

"You're kidding," Barbara stammered, visibly appalled.

"That's more than a half million dollars for a house that's falling apart," Elizabeth added, the alarm in her voice almost comical.

They all began talking at once, wanting their point to be heard, and, of course, nothing was.

Finally Ann Marie stood, all five feet of her elevated by her heels, and held her hands over her head. She began a tirade in a dialect so thick that all the other women could do was sit and stare. They couldn't be sure if they were being cussed out or advised.

Now Ann Marie's hands were braced on her rounded hips as she told them in no uncertain terms the value of property ownership, the financial rewards, tax breaks and more than anything, their dream coming true.

"We can do this. Just because the house costs that much doesn't mean we can't negotiate. Between us four we can make a solid down payment and I can work the numbers so that it won't break us." She waited for them to absorb her advice.

Their expressions slowly shifted from horror, to confusion, to understanding, to acceptance.

"I think we can do this," Barbara said, looking from one to the other. "I know we can. I have some money stashed away. Marvin made sure that I would be taken care of, and I can't think of any better way to use some of it."

"I have plenty of equity in my house," Elizabeth said, "and I'm sure not going to let that…bastard and his girlfriend get their hands on it." She gave a sharp nod of her head to emphasize her point.

"My extra income from my apartment building is just going in the bank. I'll use that," Ann Marie offered, then turned to Stephanie. "And you can toss in some of those bonuses you are always bragging about."

Stephanie jumped up, her eyes like two daggers aimed at Ann Marie. "Go to hell." She grabbed her laptop and ran out the door before anyone could react.

Ann Marie stood wide-eyed and innocent. "What did I say?"

"The same thing you always say," Barbara snapped, heading for the door. "Too much."

Barbara ran outside, catching up with Stephanie an instant before she put the key in the lock of her car door. She put her hand on her shoulder to turn her around.

"Steph, come on. You know Ann Marie doesn't mean anything." She came around to face Stephanie, who quickly turned her face away but not before Barbara saw her red eyes and tears streaming down her cheeks. "Steph, honey, what is it?"

Stephanie shook her head back and forth. "Just a really bad day, Barb, and you can't fix it. Okay?" She pulled away from Barbara's hold. "I gotta go." She sniffed hard. "I'll call you." She opened her car door and got in. "And for the record, I'm in as long as I don't have to deal with that...bitch!" She slammed the door shut and sped off, leaving Barbara to inhale a plume of exhaust fumes.

Barbara watched as Stephanie drove right past her building and kept on going.

Barbara returned to her apartment and gently closed the door. All eyes were on her when she re-entered the living room.

"She says she's in." Barbara left out the rest.

"Maybe I should call her," Ann Marie offered.

"I wouldn't do that if I were you," Elizabeth said. "Give her some space. Besides, you have an uncanny way of pissing Stephanie off."

Ann Marie mumbled something under her breath. "I can get us in to see the properties on Monday if you all agree."

"I'm off work at four on Monday," Barbara said.

"After I see my attorney I'm free." Elizabeth leaned back in her seat. "I'll talk to him about what property rights I have while I'm there."

"Good. So why don't we all meet at my office on Monday at five-thirty?"

Barbara and Elizabeth nodded in agreement.

"You should be the one to tell Stephanie," Ann Marie said to Barbara. "Unless, of course, she has one of her hot dates and can't make it." She folded her arms like a recalcitrant child and pouted.

"It's statements like those that always has you in trouble." Barbara shook her head. "You ladies hungry?"

Elizabeth stood and stretched. "No. I think I'll go home."

"Me, too," Ann Marie said. "No telling what Raquel is up to in my house."

Elizabeth and Barbara looked at each other but held their comments.

Ann Marie collected her paperwork and stuck

them back in her portfolio. She headed for the door then looked back at Elizabeth.

"Ellie, you comin', chile? I can give you a lift."

"I have my car. Thanks. Just going to use the bathroom before I leave. You go ahead. See you on Monday."

Even though they all lived on the same stretch of Morningside Drive with one or two blocks separating them, they always drove their cars to each other's homes. It was a standing joke between them.

Ann Marie shrugged. "Night then." She waved and walked out.

"Whew," Elizabeth breathed. "That got pretty ugly."

"Hmm."

"Did Stephanie say anything?"

Barbara repeated Stephanie's parting comment and Elizabeth laughed, her first for the day.

"Sometimes I have to wonder if Ann Marie is intentionally vicious or if she really doesn't know any better," Barbara commented as they walked into the kitchen.

Elizabeth took a seat at the island counter and began spinning the napkin holder on the smooth marble surface.

"I'm really glad you stopped by today." She looked up at Barbara, who was standing near the sink.

"So am I." She smiled at her friend. "Want some iced tea?"

"Sure."

She poured a glass for each of them and sat down. "So, how are you, really?"

"Other than feeling like my whole world has collapsed, I'm fine." She was pensive for a moment. "I didn't even see it happening. And I guess the question that haunts me is what did I do wrong?"

"You didn't do anything. This was Matt's choice."

"But I'm his wife. I should have noticed something."

"Well, they say the wife is always the last to know. Maybe there were signs, maybe there weren't. But the main thing is you. You have to take care of Ellie."

Elizabeth took a sip of her drink and slowly nodded her head. She pushed out a long breath. "And I think our new venture is just what I need. What we all need."

"So do I." She smiled, her thoughts coming in a rush of possibilities. "So do I."

Chapter 11

Ann Marie had decided to do some last-minute food shopping before going home. She felt kind of bad about what she'd said to Stephanie, even though every word of it was true. She couldn't understand why people got so unnerved by her. She spoke her mind. And sometimes the truth hurt, even if it wasn't intentional. The truth was, Stephanie was a corporate tramp. Didn't she admit to sleeping with her boss and lawd knows who else to get where she was in the company. Hmmph, but when she says something everyone gives her the screw face. Was she wrong?

She parked her car and went inside. As usual on a Saturday evening the megasupermarket was packed. She made quick work of picking up the items she needed and got in line.

Behind her was an older and a younger woman. They were having an intense conversation about the upcoming elections and Ann Marie was quite amazed to hear the young girl's views on the state of the world and the responsibility of politicians to their constituents. What was more amazing was that the older woman seemed truly interested in what the young woman was saying, asking probing questions and adding her own opinions. The conversation shifted from politics to hip-hop music, books and the latest fashion trends while they waited for their turn with the cashier.

"Ma, we forgot ketchup," the young woman said.

Ann Marie turned, shocked. Mother and daughter, talking like friends?

The realization unsettled Ann Marie in a way she could not quite grasp as she witnessed a smile akin to love light up the woman's face. The girl got off line, darted around shopping carts and customers then disappeared down one of the aisles.

She couldn't ever remember having a conversation with her mother about anything beyond household chores and school. In her mother's house, you listened and that was it. Children were seen and not heard and she'd raised Raquel the same way.

She put her purchases on the conveyor belt, paid with her credit card and walked out with her two plastic bags of groceries.

On the drive home, she suddenly felt lost and very alone, as if some major piece of her existence was suddenly missing and she didn't know why.

* * *

Ann Marie returned home to the aroma of stewed fish and callaloo. Her stomach growled.

Raquel was in the living room watching television and quickly turned off the TV with the remote when she heard the key in the door.

Even at the age of twenty-three she was still afraid of her mother. Not that her mother would physically harm her, but she would withhold any semblance of kindness for the smallest infraction.

All her life Raquel believed that her mother held her happiness in the palm of her hand and would crush it on a whim. She was never sure what it was that would set her mother off on one of her verbal assaults and then the silence that followed, which was far more punishing. She'd spent years trying to win her mother's love, but it was never forthcoming.

When she married Earl she believed that she was finally free, that she'd found someone to love her and make her feel worthwhile. Her fantasy was short-lived. And now, without any real friends or family to turn to, she'd come back to the one place she'd hoped never to return to—home.

"Hello, Mama." Raquel quickly got up to help Ann Marie with the bags.

Ann Marie's lips pinched into a line for a moment. "I didn't think you'd hear me with the television up so loud. All you young people are deaf."

"Sorry," Raquel murmured, even though she knew the television had been barely audible. "I prepared dinner. I can fix you a plate if you're hungry."

Ann Marie glanced around her precious space. Everything was as it should be. She released a breath of tense air.

"Maybe later." She left her bags with Raquel and went into her bedroom shutting the door behind her.

She sat on the side of her queen-size bed and took off her shoes and out of nowhere she wanted to weep. The feeling crept up from the soles of her feet and rocked her as they shot to her heart and poured from her eyes. Raquel's unexpected return into her life made her angry, sad, confused and uncertain of herself.

Raquel symbolized all that was wrong with Ann Marie, all that was incomplete. But if she could keep Raquel at a distance, out of sight and out of mind, she wouldn't have to think about anything below the surface. She wouldn't have to struggle with emotions that she didn't know what to do with. She wouldn't have to be a mother.

Chapter 12

"Ms. Moore," the nurse at the front desk of St. Ann's Nursing Home said in surprise. "We weren't expecting you."

"I know. I just needed to stop by. Is it all right if I see her? I know it's late…"

"Sure. I know it will make her happy."

"Thanks."

"You can go in. She's in her room." She handed her a pass.

Stephanie clipped the pass onto her sweater and walked down the hushed corridor. She stopped in front of room 262, knocked gently then opened the door.

Samantha sat in a chair by the window, her favorite spot. Slowly she turned her head, sensing a presence behind her. A hint of recognition lit her eyes and a crooked smile formed on her mouth.

"Hey, sweetie," Stephanie said, slowly approaching. She knelt down in front of her twin sister and took her hands. "How are you today?"

Samantha stared blankly. Stephanie didn't expect a response. Samantha never uttered more than an inappropriate giggle or unintelligible sounds.

Stephanie stroked her sister's cheek and tried not to cry. "Did you have a good day? It was so pretty outside after the rain last night."

Samantha's gaze drifted toward the window as if she may have understood, but Stephanie knew better. According to the doctors, Samantha had suffered extensive, irreversible brain damage in a car accident more than fifteen years earlier. Stephanie had been able to walk away.

Every day since, Stephanie blamed herself. She'd been the one to insist that Samantha accompany her to the party. Sam hadn't wanted to go. She was tired and wanted to study for her final exams. She had aspirations of being a doctor one day. But Stephanie, always the stronger willed of the two, convinced her. And she'd spent every waking hour since that fateful night regretting it.

So she placed her sister in the best facility that New York had to offer. Cost was no object, she'd insisted to the doctors. She would find a way to pay for her sister's care, and she did.

No one knew about her twin sister, not even the girls. It was her albatross to bear, her private penance.

"I'll come back tomorrow, okay? And maybe we can go for a walk on the grounds. Would you like that?"

Samantha looked at her sister and for an instant the unfocused eyes seemed to register and then nothing.

Stephanie swallowed over the tight knot in her throat, stood, then leaned down and kissed Samantha tenderly on the cheek. "I love you, sweetie."

Before she let her sister see her tears, she turned and hurried out of the room. She leaned back against the wall and shut her eyes. She would do whatever was necessary for Samantha. Anything.

Pulling herself together, she tugged in a long breath then walked to the reception desk, promised the nurse she would return the next day and walked out.

Yes, she would do whatever, even if it meant sleeping with Conrad until the end of time.

She drove off and headed home to wait.

Chapter 13

The last person Elizabeth expected to see when she returned home was her husband sitting in the living room as if nothing had happened.

Matthew stood when the door shut behind him.

A short breath caught in Elizabeth's chest. "What are you doing here?" She put her purse on the table and walked fully into the room.

"I came to pick up my things. But I didn't want to leave without speaking to you first."

"Oh, really. How thoughtful!" she spat out.

Matthew glanced away for a moment then back at his wife. "Can we talk?"

"I was pretty sure you'd said everything you wanted to say to me." She folded her arms.

"Ellie, we don't have to make this any harder than it already is."

"Is that right? Well, in your world, Matthew, just how hard is it? Does it keep you up at night, does it make you look in the mirror and ask yourself how you could have done this?" Her voice rose in pitch. "Does your stomach turn every time you think about throwing twenty-five years of marriage out the window? Do you think about how you've made me feel? Tell me, Matthew, how hard is it?"

Her breathing came in short rapid bursts and if she wasn't holding her arms around her waist she was certain she would fall apart.

"I'm sorry, Ell. I never meant to hurt you."

"Bull! What do you think you've done—made my day?"

Matthew heaved a sigh then ran his left hand across his face. His diamond wedding band flashed and Elizabeth's stomach twisted.

Elizabeth lifted her chin. "Are you living with her now?"

"No. I'm staying at a hotel."

Elizabeth stepped farther into the room, but kept her distance from Matthew. "Why, does the child still live at home with mommy?"

"She's thirty."

Elizabeth rolled her eyes. "What do you want to talk about? So that you can say it and get out of my house."

"I want to talk about the house."

Her eyes cinched. "What about it?"

"I want to give you enough money to…find something else. When the divorce is final, I want to move back in with Terri."

Elizabeth felt all the wind leave her lungs and she nearly doubled over with the sucker punch.

"W-hat?" she stammered.

"I want the house. I've paid for it all these years and—"

"You have lost your mind. You think your money is what kept this house and this family afloat all these years?" She arched her neck and spewed a nasty laugh. "You are a fool." She began to circle him in predatory fashion, forcing him to turn as she did. "And if you think you and your tramp girlfriend are going to move in and move me out, you are in for the fight of your life. Now, get your things out of *my* house before I call the police and have you removed."

She spun away and stormed off to the study, slamming the door behind her before she broke down and asked him to stay.

Elizabeth stood still as stone, listening to Matthew move around in the bedroom, opening and closing drawers and closets, and then silence.

She waited a few minutes more until she heard the front door close. It was only then that she released a breath. She expected tears and an overwhelming sensation of defeat and sadness.

Oddly enough, she didn't cry or feel sad or fall apart. Nor did she have any desire to run behind him. Instead, she felt strong, stronger than she'd ever felt in all her years of marriage to Matthew.

Throughout all their time together she'd let her needs and wants take a back seat to her husband's. She'd never questioned, never disagreed, never put her foot down. And now that she had, it felt damn good!

She'd been raised in the old school: a woman's place was in the home at her husband's side, and in his home he was king. It was the life she'd seen with her mother and father. They'd been married for fifty-one years. That was what she'd hoped for, for her and Matthew. Her mother and father would be stunned. They believed Matthew could do no wrong and that she was lucky to have a man like him. The twins would be devastated. They worshipped the ground their father walked on.

Elizabeth knew it would be an uphill battle to make them all believe that Matthew's infidelity wasn't her fault.

She straightened her spine. They could think what the hell they wanted. She knew the truth and truth always won out.

She checked the time on the overhead clock above the six-foot bookcase. The girls should be closing up the store in another hour. It was time she had a talk with them.

Chapter 14

With the ladies gone and plans made to meet Monday evening, Barbara had every intention of doing nothing more strenuous with her evening than watching television.

This weekend had been one for the record books. She would never have imagined hearing the things she'd heard from her friends—women she'd been

so close with for the past decade. And she would have never imagined herself sleeping with Michael, either—not that they'd done much sleeping.

She kicked off her shoes and put on her slippers then went into the kitchen to see what she could toss together for a light supper. She turned on the radio that she kept atop the fridge and hummed along with Aretha's "Ain't No Way," while she prepared a grilled-chicken salad. She added the last of the toppings and was reaching for the salad dressing when the doorbell rang.

With a slight frown, she set the bottle of Italian dressing on the counter, wiped her hands on the burnt-orange dish towel and went to the door.

She wished for the zillionth time that the landlord would get that front-door lock and the intercom fixed. Any and everybody could walk into the building. It wasn't safe.

"Who?" she asked, then took a look through the peephole. The only thing she could see was a profusion of roses in every color of the rainbow. Her heart thumped. It was either a very classy serial killer or that fine young thang. "Who?" she sang again.

"How many men do you generally have coming to your door with three dozen roses? That's the real question."

Barbara covered her mouth to hold back the screech and did a quick flash-dance step before turning the lock. She tugged in a lungful of calm, schooled her expression and as slow as she pleased, opened the door and stepped back to let Michael in.

"Good thing I'm in shape. These are heavy," he said over the crest of the blooms.

They were magnificent. Red, yellow, peach, white and a deep orange that rivaled the sunset sat regally in an enormous crystal vase.

"Michael…" She was actually speechless.

"I know I should have called first." He gently set

the vase down on the center of the coffee table then turned to her. "But I knew if I did, you'd come up with a million reasons why now was not a good time." He grinned sheepishly and walked toward her. "I don't take rejection well. Just ask my coach."

Damn, he's fine. "You're probably right…about me saying no." Her voice sounded as weak as she felt. And why did he have to make it worse by looking at her as if she held some secret that he couldn't wait to get his hands on. *Ooooh, those hands.*

"So I figured I'd bring a peace offering, to be on the safe side."

He was right up on her now. His arm snaked around her waist.

She was having trouble breathing. Lawd, please don't let me have a heart attack. Not now! "They're beautiful. I've never seen anything like you…them before."

"I want to fill your whole world with beautiful things."

His thumb massaged that spot at the base of her spine—*yeah, that spot*—right there.

"Hmm," slipped from between her lips, and her inner thighs began to tingle.

"If you let me," he continued an instant before enveloping her in a kiss that made her toes curl inside her slippers.

When Michael released her, she felt as if she'd

suddenly been dipped in cold water, and she wanted to run back into the heat of a moment ago. Good sense prevailed.

She straightened and tugged on the hem of her T-shirt to give her hands something to do besides running them up and down his body.

"I, uh, was fixing a salad." She swallowed. "You're welcome to join me."

"Sure."

He followed her into the kitchen and she suddenly wished she had on something more appealing than a faded pair of gray sweats and a T-shirt.

"You look great," he said while he took a seat at the island counter.

"And you need glasses." She walked to the fridge and took out a pitcher of iced tea.

He folded his large hands on top of the counter. "Why is it that every time I tell you how good you look or how wonderful you are you always dismiss it as though I'm handing you a line?"

She stopped short, taken off guard by the edge in his voice. Slowly she turned around to face him.

"I don't dismiss what you say."

"Of course you do and I want to know why you think you are so unworthy of a compliment?"

Barbara pressed her lips together for a moment, trying to find the words to explain the constant un-certainly that warred inside her since he'd come into her life. She pulled out a chair from beneath the counter and sat down.

"Michael, let's be honest. I'm forty-nine years old. I'll be fifty in six months, eligible for AARP for heaven's sake! And you...you're young enough to be my son. I have to color my hair every four weeks to keep the gray away. I'm slightly over-weight. I don't know a thing about rap or hip-hop. My favorite pastime is watching television. The only man in my life since I've been an adult was Marvin, my high-school sweetheart. I'm totally clueless when it comes to...dating." She blew out a breath. "Michael, my idea of excitement is having more than one drink with my girlfriends on Friday night."

"You're not that much older than me. I'll be thirty in two weeks. I like the gray...it gives you class, but if you want to cover it up, not a problem. If I don't work out on a regular basis I'd be a blimp 'cause I love to eat. I prefer classic R&B and jazz to hip-hop and rap any day. I love relaxing in front of the tube and I haven't had a steady girlfriend in five years. And like you, I enjoy a drink with the fellas to unwind, too." He looked at her with a smirk. "What else ya got?"

Barbara lowered her head and chuckled.

"So, instead of looking at all the reasons why not, look at the reasons why. I really like you, and you like me. You're intelligent and so am I—contrary to the belief that jocks are dopes. There's no question that sex between us is off the charts."

Barbara felt her face heat.

Michael reached across the table and took her left hand. He looked deep into her eyes, his expression intense and serious. "I read books, too," he said.

Barbara looked at him. The corners of his mouth quivered and she burst out laughing.

"And I can make you laugh."

She nodded and kept on chuckling. "That much is true," she managed to say. Slowly she sobered. "Mike…it's not going to be easy."

"No relationship is."

"We're from two different worlds."

"You bring me yours and I'll bring you mine." He squeezed her hand a bit tighter. "I want to get to know everything about you and I want you to know me, too. As much as I'd like what we do in bed to be no more than a booty call, I want a real relationship and I want it with you. The booty is extra."

Barbara broke up laughing again. "You do have a way with words."

"I try." He waited a beat. "I meant everything I said."

She nodded her head slowly. "I believe you."

"Well…how about it, Barbara? Can we try this thing for real?"

A million excuses ran through her head, all the reasons why the two of them were a bad idea. She was a rational woman. She thought things out. She wasn't impulsive. She knew the kinds of looks she would get and the comments that would be made about her. But she didn't care. For once in her life she was going to be impulsive, she was going to throw out her reservations. She was going to give them a chance and herself a chance at happiness again for however long it lasted.

"Okay," she said finally. "Let's try."

A smile broke out across his face that lit up the room.

"And in honor of this momentous occasion," he said ceremoniously, "I want to ask you out on our first official date, in public, this weekend."

"This weekend?" she squeaked.

He nodded. "You pick the place."

She drew in a breath. "Okay. Um, how about dinner at B. Smith's?"

"Wherever you want. Not a problem. And to wrap up the night, dancing at the Knitting Factory in the Village."

"Dancing? I haven't—"

"Danced in ages? Me neither." He grinned. "It will be an experience for both of us."

"It sure will," she said, and was actually looking forward to it. Wait until she told the girls. Hmm, dinner and dancing. She'd have to do some shopping.

Chapter 15

Elizabeth sat outside Delectables, the café and local gathering spot that her daughters owned. She was so very proud of them and all that they'd accomplished. She watched them through the plate-glass window as they jointly handled their last customer. If nothing else, those two girls were one thing that she and Matthew did right.

It was Dawne who came to the door when the customer left, and locked up behind him. Elizabeth hesitated a moment. Maybe now wasn't the right time. Maybe she should wait, at least until she spoke with her attorney about her options. But she didn't want to risk Matthew getting to them first and twisting his version of the facts. Although she was really unclear how he could polish up being an adulterer and making it palatable. But with Matthew, his charm could turn coal into diamonds with just his smile. It had been her downfall, and ever since he'd dropped the bomb on her life, she'd begun to wonder how many others may have succumbed to Matthew's charm.

She turned off the ignition and got out, setting the alarm with the remote as she walked to the entrance. She tapped lightly on the door. Her daughters' faces beamed with delight when they saw her.

"Mom," they chorused.

"What are you doing here?" Dawne asked, putting her arm around her mother's shoulder and ushering her inside.

Desiree pushed her twin playfully aside. "What kind of question is that? Mom is always welcome."

Dawne stuck her tongue out at her sister. "Hungry, Mom? We can whip you up our specialty, the Delectable veggie burger—on the house, of course." She giggled.

"No, sugar. I'm not hungry." She stopped in the center of the shop and turned to look at her daughters. She took their hands. "I need to talk to you girls."

Their identical expressions of alarm set Elizabeth's pulse flying. She pulled in a breath. "Let's sit down."

"Mom, you're scaring me," Dawne said.

"You're not sick, are you?" Desiree asked, slow sitting down at the table. Dawne followed suit.

Elizabeth put her purse down on the wood surface and sat down. "No, I'm not sick. Nothing like that."

Dawne exhaled a sigh of relief, then her eyes widened. "Is it Dad?"

"Yes, but not what you think." She paused a beat. "Your dad and I are getting divorced."

A heavy silence descended on the rectangular room. Each and every sound from the street seemed to be amplified in stereo as the trio sat in utter stillness.

Desiree's expression slowly hardened. "Is it because of that woman at his office?" she said, barely moving her lips.

"Desi!" Dawne admonished.

Desiree flashed her sister a look. "I knew it!"

"What did you know?" Elizabeth asked.

Desiree sighed. "I went to Dad's office a couple of months ago. I wanted to surprise him with our new recipe—"

"A vegan carrot cake," Dawne cut in.

"Can I tell my story, please? Anyway, I wanted to surprise him, like I was saying, so I went straight to his office. And when I walked in, without knocking, like I always do, Dad and Terri sprung apart like they'd been shot with a bolt of lightning."

Elizabeth felt nauseous. *That bastard.*

"They were both very nervous and Terri raced out of there as if the starting bell had gone off. She couldn't look me in the eye. When I asked him what that was all about he said she'd been crying—some nonsense about an ill family member and he was only comforting her."

Dawne sucked her teeth with disgust. "Yeah, right." She folded her arms.

Desiree leaned forward. "Well, is it her? Is she the reason?"

Elizabeth momentarily closed her eyes and nodded her head in agreement. "Yes," she murmured. "Your father said he's in love with her."

"Oh, I have a word for what it is, and it ain't love," Dawne spat.

"Mom, it's not your fault. I know you and I know that's what you're thinking," Desiree offered. "It's Dad's loss."

"Exactly, Mom. If that's what he wants to do, then as much as I love my father, I'd say let him go. You deserve to be happy and not living with someone who is sneaking around."

"And we're not kids anymore. You don't have to worry about staying together because of us," Desiree said.

"Exactly," Dawne concurred.

Elizabeth looked at her daughters, the two beautiful little babies who'd grown into beautiful, successful, intelligent women, and her heart filled with so much love for them it was enough to get her through anything. She swallowed over the big knot in her throat and blinked back tears.

"Thank you. Thank you both. I...I didn't know what to expect when I told you. I know how much you both love and adore your dad."

"Mom, we love and adore you, too." Desiree grinned.

"Yeah, even when you still nag us," Dawne teased.

"So," Desiree, always direct, began. "What are you planning to do?"

Elizabeth smiled for the first time since she arrived. "Well, the other night me and the girls came up with this brilliant idea…."

Chapter 16

Excitement coursed through Barbara all day at work. She should be exhausted, but instead she felt revitalized, as if she'd been given a shot of happy juice. She and Michael had talked for hours, well into the early morning, until they'd both fallen asleep curled in each other's arms on her bed. He told her about his life growing up in North Carolina as the only boy in a family of four sisters.

"I spent the bulk of my growing-up years waiting to get in the bathroom and giving the evil eye to wannabe boyfriends."

Barbara laughed at the images. "I was an only child," she'd confessed. "I always wondered what it would be like to have sisters and brothers. I guess that's why I'm so attached to my friends. They're the sisters I never had."

"I'd like to meet them."

Her eyes widened for a moment. "You would?"

"Of course. And I want you to meet my friends, too."

She was shaking her head as she spoke. "Mike... meeting your friends..."

"I want to show you off. I want my friends to know how lucky I am to have found you."

"Let's give *us* some time first, okay?"

Reluctantly he agreed. "You say when."

"It won't be long, promise. I told my friends about you already."

"What did you tell them?"

"You really don't want to know."

"Yes, I do. What did you tell them?"

"That you were one of my patients and that you were young enough to be my son and that...I really like you."

"What did they say about the age thing?"

"They all told me to go for it. That you only live once."

He grinned. "I like them already."

Barbara felt good inside thinking about the big step she'd taken with Michael. She'd been stopped several times by staff members on how "glowing" she appeared. Guess there was some truth in the saying that happiness made you glow.

Before he'd left her apartment, shortly before dawn, he'd told her that he had to go out of town for a few days but would be back in plenty of time for their date. He had a meeting with his coach and the team doctor in Florida who wanted him to begin a restricted training program to see how the knee was coming along.

When he told her he would be going away for a few days, she actually felt sad, maybe *disappointed* was a better word. Sure she was glad that he had come far enough to go back into training, but she would miss him. The time they'd spent together was balm for her soul. She felt complete and looked forward to the days ahead.

She took a stack of towels from the supply cabinet as she prepared for her next patient. The reality was, she mused as she placed the towels on the exercise table, if she planned on continuing a relationship with Michael she would have to get used to his traveling, being away from her for weeks, sometimes months, at a time. She sighed and pressed her lips together in thought. Was that what she wanted—a part-time lover?

Her years of marriage to Marvin had molded her in a way. She enjoyed the daily routine, of waking up next to her husband, always knowing she had a "date" for the holidays, someone always there at the end of a hard day to listen to her, and for her to be a shoulder, as well. Could it ever be that way again? Could it ever be that way with Michael? It would be several years before he would hang up his sneakers. Was she willing to wait?

Whoa, she was getting way ahead of herself. They'd made no lasting commitment to each other. And if she knew nothing else, great sex didn't a solid relationship make.

"Barbara, your next patient is here. Mrs. Wells."

Barbara turned and forced a smile. "I'm ready. Send her in."

Mrs. Wells was one of her favorite patients. She was a young ninety years old and had broken her hip in a horseback riding fall nearly six months earlier. Unlike most senior patients with that kind of injury, Mrs. Wells was determined not to become an invalid. She'd made a miraculous recovery and was walking with a cane, something that really "pissed her off," her feisty patient would say. "Makes people think I'm old."

Barbara smiled for real when Veronica Wells walked into the room, head held high, back straight, accompanied by her husband, Herb. They'd been married sixty years and both swore they had another sixty in them.

"And how is my favorite patient today?" Barbara beamed.

"She's still pissed off," Herb announced.

Veronica elbowed him in the side. "I'd stop being pissed off if I could toss this infernal cane."

Barbara came over to help her to the table, but Veronica waved her off.

"I can manage." She set her cane aside and took off her stylish trench coat. She looked up at Barbara, placed her forefinger beneath Barbara's chin and turned her face from side to side. Veronica's right brow rose an inch. "New lover?" she asked, unabashed.

Barbara blinked several times while the question ricocheted around in her head looking for traction.

"You can tell me. I've been around long enough to have heard everything and I can tell when a woman has had great sex, a mile away."

"Veronica!" Herb warned. "You have to excuse her, Barbara. She hasn't taken her medication this morning. She's a little crazier than usual."

Veronica turned to her husband and clucked her tongue. "Can you honestly stand there, Herb, and tell me that this woman doesn't look radiant? And what is the one thing that puts a glow in a woman's cheeks and a secret sparkle in her eyes? Great sex!" She nodded her head definitively. "Don't you always say that to me after we've done it?"

Herb shook his head in surrender. "I think I'll wait outside."

"Good! Let us girls talk." She waved him off, then turned her attention back to Barbara. "Is he cute at least?"

Barbara started to laugh, a deep soul-stirring laugh of release. "Yes, very," she was finally able to say.

"That's a start," Veronica said, waving a finger in

Barbara's face. "All that stuff about 'in the dark' is for the birds. You have to turn the lights on sometime and you want to be able to take him out in public." She chuckled. "Help me with this zipper." She turned her back to Barbara, who unzipped her dress.

As usual, Veronica was clad in the latest Victoria's Secret undies. Barbara smiled to herself. Mrs. Wells was something else. She helped her up onto the table and prepared her for her exam and massage.

"Well…" Veronica questioned.

"Well what?" Barbara braced Veronica's hip in her right hand and lifted her leg with her left.

"Who is he?"

"Tell me when it hurts," Barbara said, avoiding the question. She raised the leg a bit higher. "He's just a friend," she confessed.

"And…is he any good?"

"Veronica!"

"Well, is he?"

Barbara pressed her lips together as visions of her and Michael danced in her head. "Yes," she said on a breath. "Very."

Veronica clapped with delight. "That's what I like to hear. So what's the problem?"

"Why do you think there's a problem?"

"The hesitation in your eyes. Is he married?"

"No."

"Babies?"

"No."

"Gay?"

"Definitely not!"

"So what is it?"

"He's...much younger than I am."

"And what's wrong with that?"

"Nothing, it's just—"

"Happiness only comes around a couple of times. And when it does, we have to snatch it and hold on to it for as long as we can. I know."

Barbara lowered Veronica's leg, went to the cabinet and took out the massage oils. She returned to the table. "How do you know?" she asked, really needing to hear some wisdom.

"Maybe you don't know this, but Herb is not my first husband. Divorced that S.O.B. and took him for everything he had." She shrugged. "And when I finally decided to get back in the market, Herb came along. Young, handsome and sexy. Just the way I like them."

Barbara giggled.

"No one thought it would work. That Herb was a rebound lover and too young for me. But we proved them all wrong."

Barbara's interest perked up. "Too young?" She applied the oils to the incredibly smooth skin and began to rub.

"Herb is fifteen years younger than me. Snatched him right out of his mama's house." She giggled.

"And I've never regretted one minute and neither has he." She angled her head to look at Barbara. "Is that it? He's younger than you?"

Slowly Barbara nodded. "Almost twenty years."

Veronica slapped the table in glee. "Now, *that's* what I'm talking about. And what he lacks in experience he makes up for in energy. Keeps you young. Look at me. If I was married to some old coot do you think I would still keep myself in the shape that I'm in? I don't want any of these young hussies getting their hands on my Herb."

Barbara had to admit, Veronica was in excellent shape. She had the toned body of a forty-year-old woman, give or take a few years, and she had the personality and mentality to go along with her youthful appearance.

"So you think I should pursue it?"

"I sure as hell do. Ride the wave." She giggled.

All the way home, Barbara thought of her scandalous conversation with Veronica. Maybe she was right. She should just enjoy it and stop being so conventional. Go with the flow, as the kids would say. Even the girls said to go for it.

At the red light, it hit her. If Veronica could do it so could she.

When the light changed she made a left and headed toward the shopping strip on historic One Hundred and Twenty-fifth Street.

If she was going to cross that line she was going to do it in style and give Michael something to look at while she was at it.

She found a metered parting space and crossed the street. Taking a deep breath of resolve she pulled open the doors of the newly established Victoria's Secret.

It had been a while since she'd used her credit card on something for herself. She was long overdue.

Barbara pulled up in front of her building nearly two hours later. She took her four pink-and-white stripped signature bags from the car and practically skipped to her front door.

She grinned as she put her key in the lock. Wait until Michael saw her in these. Yeah, go with the flow. After all, it wasn't as if they were planning on marriage.

Chapter 17

Stephanie was just turning off her computer when there was a knock on her office door. She looked up and her stomach did a quick dive to her toes then rose to her throat.

"Thought we could get together for drinks."

"I have plans." She shoved a folder into her desk.

Conrad stepped in and shut the door behind him. "With who?"

She stared him in the eye, certain that he wouldn't cause a scene in the office. "I don't think that's any of your business. I said I have plans."

"Another man?"

She put her right hand on her hip. "Go home to your wife and kids." She picked up her purse then her jacket from the back of her chair. She started toward the door.

"You're upset about the other night. Look, I'm sorry I didn't get back. I got tied up."

"It really doesn't matter, Conrad," she said,

weary from the direction of the conversation that was going nowhere.

He grabbed her arm when she reached for the door. "I'll make it up to you."

"Not necessary. Good night."

He lowered his head so that his lips met her ear. "We'll talk about this again." He let her go and she walked out.

Stephanie walked down the corridor toward the elevator. Her legs were shaking. This couldn't go on. It just couldn't. She pressed the down button. She had to find a way out and still be able to take care of Samantha. She looked down the corridor and saw Conrad talking with one of the associates at the reception desk.

On the surface Conrad Hendricks was the greatest guy on the planet. At least to those who didn't really know him. He was handsome, intelligent, funny when necessary and from the outside seemed like a real family man. But she knew differently. The elevator doors opened. Conrad glanced in her direction and smiled an instant before she stepped on and the doors swished closed behind her.

Their illicit affair began innocently enough, she recalled as the elevator made its slow descent from the fifteenth floor. He'd called her into his office after she'd landed a major client for the firm.

"Great job, Stephanie," he'd begun after offering her a seat.

"Thank you." Getting noticed by the head of the firm was something that she'd diligently worked toward from the day she joined the company. Now she was finally being recognized for all of her hard work.

"I was going over your file," he continued. "Quite impressive. You are probably one of the most underrated rainmakers in the company." He leaned back against the plush cushions of his executive leather chair and looked her over. Suddenly he leaned forward, giving her an intent stare. "In this business you can only survive when you stay at the top of your game, draw in the big names and keep them in the public eye." He folded his hands atop his desk. "My business is surrounding myself with dynamic people, those who have the charisma and the drive to get to and stay at the top—no matter what that takes."

Stephanie swallowed and adjusted herself in the seat, wondering where this conversation was heading.

"Beginning on Monday, you will move to the corner office. You'll have your own assistant and you will be my right hand."

A hot flash raced through her, making her head pound. Was he saying what she thought he was saying? A major promotion? Conrad Hendricks's assistant? She must be dreaming.

"You look surprised. You don't think you deserve it?"

She blinked herself back to reality. "Yes, yes, of

course I think I deserve it," she stammered with excitement.

The corner of his full mouth curved upward. "That's better. I'll be turning over some of our bigger accounts to you in the coming months, just to see how well you really handle pressure."

"No problem." She sat up straighter in her seat. "I'm ready."

"Glad to hear it." He stood. "I think this calls for a celebration. If you don't have plans I'd like to take my new assistant out to dinner. Tomorrow, about six."

She swallowed. "Thank you. That would be wonderful."

"Good. I'll make a formal announcement to the staff in the morning." He extended his hand.

Stephanie stood and shook his hand.

"Firm grip. I like that." He released her. "That's it then."

"Yes, sir."

"From now on you can call me Conrad."

She nodded. "Conrad."

"Much better. We're going to be working very closely together and formalities only make for more tension." He smiled. "Tomorrow, then. Have a good evening, Stephanie."

"Thank you. Thank you for having faith in me."

He walked her to the door and held it open. "One

thing I must warn you about. I expect results. I don't take kindly to failures."

"That won't be a problem."

"Good." He stepped aside to let her pass. "Travel safely."

"You, too."

That was nearly two years ago. And for a good while it was strictly business between them. She worked hard, grueling hours and many weekends. They had brainstorming sessions sometimes into the wee hours of the morning. It was exhausting, but she never faltered and her bank account bore the fruits of her labor.

It was maybe a year into her new job. She and Conrad were working late. The office was empty. Even the cleaning crew had gone for the night. They'd ordered Chinese from the local restaurant and had finally taken a break to eat.

"I really like all that you've been giving to the company, Stephanie," he said before lifting his fork filled with lo mein.

She smiled and took a sip of her tea. "I told you when you gave me this position that I would give it my all."

"That you have." He looked at her for a long moment. "There's something about dynamic, self-assured women that has always intrigued me." He paused. "You intrigue me in more ways than one."

She nearly choked.

He looked sheepish. He lowered his gaze. "I know I have no right to say this to you. I know it's inappropriate, but I'm going to say it, anyway." He looked into her eyes. "I have feelings for you. Deep feelings. I've been struggling to keep them on the back burner, but I can't, not anymore."

He got up and came around to her side of the small, rectangular worktable. He stood in front of her. Slowly he took the cup from her hand and put it on the table. He took her hands and pulled her to her feet. Her heart was racing so fast she began to feel dizzy.

"I'm going to kiss you. I want to see what that's like."

And he did, slow, tender and long as if he'd loved her all his life and finally had the chance to show it. Stephanie felt herself melting into the comfort and security of his embrace, giving herself up to the sensual kiss.

She didn't protest when he cupped her behind and pulled her closer. She didn't stop him when he unbuttoned her blouse and loosened her bra. She didn't say "no" when he backed her onto the couch and hiked up her skirt. She didn't push him away when he removed her panties and pleasured her until she trembled. She didn't say "we can't" when she felt him enter her.

Instead, she thought about what "no," "stop," "we can't," would do to her career. Instead, she thought about how good he was making her feel. Instead, she thought that maybe he really did care, that maybe he would leave his wife and kids, that maybe he'd marry her and she'd never have to worry about how she would take care of Samantha.

So she gave him what he wanted and what she needed—time and time and time again.

When she focused, she was the only one left on the elevator. The doors were just about to close when she hurried off.

Her eyes burned as she fought back tears of regret and shame. Walking quickly with her head down, she went to the employees parking garage and got into her car. For several moments she sat behind the wheel taking deep breaths in the hope that it would quell the sinking sensation she had in the pit of her stomach.

She had to find a way out of this pit she'd fallen into. This was not who she was, no matter what Ann Marie thought or said. Sure, she may have played up her associations with celebrities and high-octane executives, but it was all smoke and mirrors. She'd dated them but she'd never bedded them. It was all for show and her twisted way of making herself appear important and wanted just like her friends. Ellie had her husband and her kids to brag about, Ann Marie had her man and Barbara had Marvin until he passed. All she had was her fancy job and a secret sister. But who would believe her now, especially after her confession to the girls about Conrad?

Stephanie put her car in gear and headed out of the garage. *Put on a happy face,* she told herself as she snatched a glance of her reflection in the mirror. The girls were waiting.

Chapter 18

Ann Marie darted from the real-estate office where she worked. She wanted to go home before her meeting with Barbara, Ellie and Stephanie—if Stephanie showed up—and change clothes.

She was feeling content and quite smug about putting together the potential deal. True, the building she had her eye on needed a ton of work, but the end results would be well worth it. It had always been a dream of hers to own a business. She made a pretty penny as a broker, but there was nothing like raking in the bucks for yourself.

As her luck would have it, she found a parking space right in front of her door. Her mood lifted another notch, that is until she put her key in the door and her real reality was there to greet her.

She put her leather portfolio down on the table in the foyer. Tugging in a breath, she walked inside. Water was running in the kitchen. She headed in that direction.

When she stood in the doorway of the kitchen, Raquel was at the sink washing dishing. For a moment, Ann Marie stood there watching her, listening to the sniffling that rose above the sound of water splashing against the pots and pans. Every now and again Raquel would use her sleeve to wipe her eyes. Then suddenly Raquel lowered her head and her shoulders heaved up and down as the painful sobs drowned out the sound of running water.

Ann Marie felt paralyzed. Not only could she not seem to make her feet move toward her daughter, her mind couldn't process what her eyes witnessed. When movement and reason returned, Ann Marie turned away and as silently as she'd entered she went to her room, thankful for the background noises that drowned out her cowardly escape.

Once inside her bedroom she eased her door shut and closed her eyes. What kind of mother was she? How could she see her daughter in apparent pain and do nothing to ease it? Was she that callous, that empty inside? The muscles of her stomach tensed.

She tugged in a deep breath of resolve and moved away from the door. Raquel was a grown woman she reasoned, not a small child with a bruised knee. Raquel would work out whatever problem she had on her own, just as she had been forced to do over the years. Who was ever there to help her? No one. Not a bloody soul.

Ann Marie moved across the room, taking off her

suit as she did. She changed into a button-down sky-blue oxford shirt and a pair of black Donna Karan slacks. She stepped into her favorite loafers, took up her purse, grabbed her black waist-length leather jacket and headed back out. She eased past the kitchen and was just about to reach the front door when Raquel called out to her.

"Mama, I didn't hear you come in."

Ann Marie turned. "Oh, yes, I'm kind of in a hurry. I have a meeting." She saw the red-rimmed eyes and trembling mouth. She licked her lips and forced a smile. "I should be back in a couple of hours."

Raquel nodded. "I'll fix dinner."

"Oh, don't worry about me. I'll probably grab something while I'm out." She turned to leave once again.

"Mama."

Ann Marie stopped with her hand on the knob. "Yes?"

"Why can't you love me?"

Ann Marie's stomach rose to her throat, strangling her, keeping the words from escaping from her loose lips. She forced it back down. "Don't be silly, chile." She opened the door and walked out, shutting it firmly behind her and separating her from the question that haunted her daily.

Elizabeth got behind the wheel of her Mercedes and headed over to the building to meet the girls. The better part of the afternoon had been spent in her attorney's office going over her bank account, all the documents that she and Matthew jointly signed and what her options were. She smiled wickedly. If Matthew thought he was going to buy her out and put her in the street he had another think coming. And now that she knew she had the support of her daughters, the sky was the limit. She hummed all the way to One Hundred and Twenty-fourth Street. If things worked out the way she envisioned, Matthew Lewis could put his head between his legs and kiss his ass goodbye! She laughed out loud just thinking about it.

Barbara was the first to arrive, still in her work uniform. She paced outside in front of the building that Ann Marie swore up and down was a diamond in the rough. Well, she was no expert on building rehab, but even Stevie Wonder could see that this place needed a lot more than a little fixing up.

Did she really want to sink the money that Marvin had left her in what was obviously a money pit? She glanced up at the facade. The windows were broken and the ones that weren't were boarded up. The grass and weeds in the small front yard rose with threatening determination past the ground-floor windows. The parlor floor door that led to the upper floors from outside had a chain lock around it, bringing to mind a dozen movies featuring the haunted house. If the outside looked this bad, she didn't want to entertain what the inside resembled. A shiver went through her. This definitely had to be the "before" picture, as it in no way resembled the building that Ann Marie had showed them and raved about.

Barbara glanced up and down the street. The block that the house sat on was relatively quiet, tree-lined with two small businesses: a Caribbean restaurant and a dry cleaner, one on each side of the long street.

She had to admit, it was an ideal location. Right around the corner was everything you could want: shopping, restaurants, bakeries, the train station within walking distance and One Hundred and Twenty-fifth Street was a stone's throw away. Hue Man and Nubian Heritage bookstores were also nearby. She looked at the building again and shook her head. She was going to strangle Ann Marie.

A car horn blew, drawing her attention to the street. It was Elizabeth. Barbara waved and leaned against the rickety iron fence while Elizabeth parked her car.

"Hey, girl," Elizabeth greeted, and kissed Barbara on the cheek. She looked up at the building and frowned with dismay. "Tell me this is not the building."

"Unless both of us have the address wrong, this is it."

"Oh, my goodness." Elizabeth stepped closer. "It looks like it needs to be condemned."

"I know," Barbara sighed. "Oh, here comes Steph. She's going to flip."

"I'm surprised she showed up," Elizabeth said in a pseudo whisper.

"Hmm. Expect fireworks."

"Hey, ladies." Stephanie kissed Barbara's and Elizabeth's cheeks. Her right brow arched. "I know this ain't the building."

Barbara and Stephanie nodded.

"Aw hell naw!" She folder her arms and began tapping her foot against the cracked pavement. "Unless there's gold up in there, she ain't getting a dime from me." She shook her head back and forth, her weave whipping across her back.

"Let's give it a chance," Barbara offered, but she wasn't feeling it, either.

Just then Ann Marie pulled up. She saw the trio in front of the house and their expressions ranged from distressed to outrage. She would have her work cut out for her, but she was confident that she could pull it off. She parked her car and got out.

The instant she approached, she held up her hand to stave off what she was sure would be a barrage of negativity.

"Before you all say one word, all I ask is that you reserve your comments until after we go through the house." She looked from one to the other. "Agreed?"

Reluctantly they each nodded their heads in turn.

"Great, come on. I have the keys." She pushed open the creaky front gate and walked toward the ground-floor entrance. After juggling with several keys she found the right one and opened the door. "Watch your step," she warned and led the way.

The trio trailed closely behind her.

When they stepped inside, even in the dim dusty interior, the majesty of the house shone through. The entry foyer opened to a long mahogany staircase. To the right was what was once a grand ballroom. The tops of the windows were stained glass, hardwood-parquet flooring ran throughout. A massive fireplace with an enormous mirror was the centerpiece of the room, accented by a crystal chandelier. The wooden archway led to another sitting room with yet another fireplace and a built-in wood-and-glass étagère. Beyond was another room that looked out onto a surprisingly large backyard. To the left was a kitchen the size of which was only seen on the Martha Stewart cooking show.

Ann Marie could feel their awe, heard it in the soft sighs and gasps of delight. "Let's go upstairs."

On the parlor floor were three large rooms with sweeping archways and sliding mahogany doors and all the original touches of historic brownstones, from the intricate molding to the cathedral ceilings. Along the hallway was a master bathroom.

"There's more," Ann Marie said, and took them up another flight of stairs while she pointed out the amenities.

Here was another small kitchen and two large adjoining rooms with another bathroom tucked away at the end of the hallway. A stately mantelpiece was the focal point of the hallway.

"This is one of the few four-story brownstones," Ann Marie offered, "and it has a livable attic, as well."

She took them up to the next floor, which also had three smaller rooms complete with all the elegant touches and a nice-size alcove that could be used for a variety of things.

"Let's check out the attic and then we can talk," Ann Marie said.

The attic was so much larger than the women expected. It had two bedrooms, a full bath and a small kitchen.

Ann Marie turned toward them with an "I told you so" smile on her lips. "Well, what do you think?"

The trio began talking all at once, saying how exquisite, beautiful, incredible it was.

Now to the real business, Ann Marie thought as they poured out their accolades. "As I said, it does need work. It is an old house, with all the original wiring. Many of the floorboards are loose, the sliding doors are off their hinges in some of the rooms, windows need to be replaced in the entire building. The stairs will have to be redone, the ceilings replastered where they were damaged by water and most, if not all, of the plumbing must be replaced." She took a breath. "And as I said the other night, the roof has to be replaced, as well." She looked from one to the other.

Barbara looked around, her eyes sweeping the space, taking snapshots in her head of what she'd seen. "I think if we can get it, we should."

"I can already see what we can do with each of the rooms," Elizabeth said. "And the kitchen downstairs is a cook's dream."

"As much as I ever hate to admit that you're right, you are," Stephanie conceded. "This place is a palace in disguise."

Ann Marie clapped her hands in delight. "So... we're going to go for it?"

"Yes!" they chorused.

"Great! First thing tomorrow, I'll start working up the numbers. I'm going to have to get all of your information to run the credit checks and get an idea from each of you how much you are willing to invest. Deal?"

"Deal!" They all joined hands.

"This is going to be awesome," Barbara said, imagining herself as a business owner, giving massage therapy to a stream of handsome men.

"I'm so excited," Elizabeth sighed, thinking that

for the first time in forty-two years she would actually be out on her own.

Stephanie nodded slowly. "Yes, ladies, I think we hit pay dirt." She was already envisioning the PR campaign she would put together to get the business off the ground.

"Did we ever decide on a name for our daring enterprise?" Ann Marie asked.

"I have just the thing," Barbara said. She held her hands up and slowly spread them left to right in dramatic fashion. "Pause for Men."

"'Where time has no limits,' could be the tagline," Stephanie added.

"I love it," Elizabeth giggled.

"Then, Pause for Men it is," Ann Marie concurred.

They put their hands one atop the other. "To success," Barbara said.

"Success!"

"I think this calls for a drink," Stephanie said.

"To drinks!" they chimed and headed out.

"Or three," Ann Marie giggled as she locked the doors behind them and opened the gateway to a new future for them all.

"Why don't we stop by Delectables?" Elizabeth asked once they were outside. "The girls can fix us a nice healthy dinner before we ply ourselves with booze. Besides, I'm so excited I can't wait to tell them."

"Sounds like a plan," Barbara said, walking

toward her car. "I haven't seen the twins in a while."

"I'm open." Stephanie took her car keys from her purse. "No one is waiting up for me."

"I'm game. I'll meet you all there." Ann Marie got behind the wheel of her Lexus. "Then we can decide where we want to go for drinks."

The quartet pulled off and met up shortly afterward at Delectables.

"Oh, my goodness," Dawne squealed when her mother and friends came through the door. "It has to be a special occasion to get all my favorite ladies here at one time."

"It is," Elizabeth said, barely able to contain her excitement.

"Well, come on in," Desiree said. "Have a seat. We were just getting ready to close, but we can certainly whip something up for you."

"Yes, we're starved," Barbara said, hugging each of her goddaughters in turn.

Once the ladies were settled and their orders taken, they all sat around a large circular table sipping smoothies until their food was ready.

"So…" Desiree began. "How long are you going to keep us in suspense?"

The ladies looked at one another with Cheshire cat grins on their faces.

"You go ahead and tell them," Ann Marie said to Elizabeth.

Elizabeth took a breath. "Well," she began…

"This is so exciting," Dawne said.

"When are you going to get the house and how can we help?" Desiree asked.

"I'm going to put the paperwork in first thing in the morning," Ann Marie said. "Then we can take it from there."

"Wow, a building full of physically fit, handsome men," Dawne said on a sigh, her gaze drifting happily off.

Barbara laughed. "Our sentiments exactly. And you two can provide the healthy meals that our healthy men will be craving once I'm through with them."

"What more could an eligible girl ask for?" Desiree said.

Ann Marie sat in momentary silence watching the love exchanged between Elizabeth and her daughters and wished that she could muster up just a semblance of it for her own daughter. Why couldn't she? This question plagued her countless times. Why?

So this was family life, Stephanie thought as she began to eat her plate of grilled salmon and seasoned yellow rice that was put in front of her. There was a time when having children of her own was the furthest thing from her mind. And the longer she stayed under the influence of Conrad, the more dismal her chances became as her biological clock was set for alarm mode. Even the bitch Ann Marie had a child, not that she deserved one…but still. How fair was that?

Barbara looked at her goddaughters with pride. She could still remember them as tiny infants in their bassinets. And now they were grown women with a thriving business and the whole world at their fingertips. It was the one thing she'd regretted during her marriage to Marvin—that they'd never had kids. They falsely believed that they had time. Ha, time. Time could be your friend or foe. It was too late for her, that much she knew. But at least she could live vicariously through Dawne and Desiree, whom she showered with all the love she would have if she'd had children of her own. The thought of children brought Michael zooming to the forefront of her mind. He was young, eligible and childless. At some point, if their relationship continued, he'd want more from her than a hot night in bed and stimulating conversation.

Chapter 19

With more than a bit of reluctance and a few drinks under her belt, Ann Marie returned home. When she stepped inside, the house was quiet.

Good, Raquel was asleep. She tiptoed to her room and gently closed the bedroom door. Flipping on the light, the first thing she saw was her reflection in the mirror, staring back at her with accusation. Quickly she turned away.

She was not a bad person. She wasn't, she thought as she slowly undressed. The only person she knew how to be was herself and it was up to others to either accept who she was or they could go to hell for all she cared.

She sat down on the side of the bed and out of nowhere tears of shame and uncertainty slid from her eyes. Why couldn't she open her heart, why couldn't she love the way she'd seen love displayed? Would she ever really feel it for anyone—even her own daughter? Would she ever have that light in her eyes that she saw sparkle in Elizabeth's when she looked at her daughters, or Barbara's when she talked about her life with Marvin, or even Stephanie's when she spoke of her accomplishments?

At times, she believed she was totally empty inside, devoid of feelings, and she had no idea what to do about it. And as much as she enjoyed Phil, even he was unable to summon that spark that she so desperately sought to feel.

Maybe this new venture would put the zip in her life that she was searching for, give her something to make her forget about all that she was not. But what if it didn't?

She slipped between her cool sheets, wishing that Phil was with her. At least their rather exuberant sexcapades would keep her mind and body busy. That was another dilemma she faced. He would be back any day now. Somehow she needed to figure out what to do about Raquel, especially since Phil didn't know anything about her.

The following morning, Ann Marie awoke tired and bleary-eyed. She peeked at the bedside clock and groaned. It was already eight. Generally by this time, she would have had her workout at the gym or at least would have run around the track in the community park, showered and be ready to walk out the door for work.

With more than a little effort she pulled herself out of bed and dragged her tired limbs into the bathroom.

She turned on the shower full blast and while the bathroom filled with steam she brushed her teeth.

Today she would put together all the paperwork to get the house off the market and get the process rolling. Whether the ladies knew it or not, as lousy as the house looked on the outside, there was someone out there willing to outbid them. She needed to get a lock on it and fast.

Feeling better, she took her shower, dressed and hurried out to the office. There was no sign of Raquel, which was probably a good thing. At least for now she wouldn't have to look into Raquel's sad and accusing eyes.

She signed heavily as she got behind the wheel of her car. At some point she was going to have to deal with the Raquel situation and soon. But for now, she had more pressing things on her mind. She turned on the radio and hummed along with Chaka Khan's "I'm Every Woman."

Chapter 20

Barbara felt uncharacteristically bold today. So much so that she broke her rule and called Michael, inviting him to join her for a quick lunch. He was due to leave town and she had an overwhelming desire to see him before he jetted away for a few days. She didn't want to wait until their "date night." She got her jacket and purse and hurried out to meet him in front of the hospital for lunch.

The moment she pushed through the glass doors she saw him standing there and her heart did a little dance in her chest. Wow, the man was fine, no question about it, and from the second looks that he was getting from passing women they knew it, too. His celebrity status might have had something to do with it, but he was still f-i-n-e. And he was all hers.

"Hi."

He turned in her direction and a smile as bright as sunshine spread across that wonderful mouth of his. Down, girl, down.

He walked up to her, slid his arm around her waist and kissed her lightly on the cheek. "You look great."

"And you have got to be kidding," she said, followed by a girlish giggle.

"If I think you look good, you look good." He squeezed her waist. "Where to? Do you have someplace in mind? I know you only have an hour."

"I was thinking we could go to the little bistro around the corner. The food is pretty good and they're fast."

"Lead the way."

As they headed down the block, Michael asked, "Not to stare a gift horse in the mouth, but to what do I owe the pleasure of lunch with you during working hours?"

She glanced up at him and her heart did that thing again. "I figured since I was making some changes in my life, this should be one of them."

"Changes? What kind of changes?"

"I'll tell you all about it during lunch."

He took her hand and heat shot up her arm. "I love a woman of mystery."

Once they were seated and the waitress had taken their orders, Barbara pulled her chair closer to the table.

"I know I've been a real prude when it came to me and you seeing each other…" She paused. "I've really been giving it a lot of thought lately." She looked him square in the eye. "I really like you, Michael. More than I thought I would or could. And…I don't want us to be a secret anymore. I want the world to see how happy I am."

The right corner of his mouth curved up into a grin. "Persistence is a virtue," he said. "I figured if I could hang in there long enough to wear you down, you'd have to give in." He chuckled and so did she. "But seriously—" he reached across the table and took her hand "—I'm glad, really glad. I want us to do things together, share things together and not just in the dark. The sex is out of this world, but you mean more to me than that."

"Really?"

"Yeah, really. Since I've been with you, I can feel myself changing, too, becoming more settled, more focused. I want you in my life, Barbara. It's as simple as that."

She lowered her head as heat flushed her face. "I want you in mine, too," she murmured.

He tipped her chin up with the pad of his forefinger. "Now, tell me, what other life changes have you made?"

She smiled. "I'm going into business, the spa business, with three of my friends."

His eyes widened with surprise. "Get out. For real?"

She nodded. "Yep. We found a property and everything right in Harlem. The building needs some work but…"

"That is great. I mean it. Tell me all about it. What's the plan?"

Barbara laid out the plan of having an exclusive day spa for men only. She told him what services would be offered, the screening process and how they planned to drum up business. "We're calling it Pause for Men."

Michael leaned back and chuckled from deep in his gut. "You women are going to have a lock on all the men."

She winked. "That's the point. At least one of them," she qualified.

"So how soon do you plan to open?"

"Hmm, a lot depends on getting the property and then the contractors to make all the repairs that are needed. She went down the list of things that had to be done.

"Hmm, all doable. I actually know some great contractors that I can recommend if you want."

"Sure. I'll let the ladies know."

Michael nodded. "So you're going to be a businesswoman. I like that. There's nothing sexier than a determined woman."

A tingle vibrated between her legs from the low timbre of his voice. "Is that right?"

"Yeah, it is. A real turn-on."

"Maybe I'll let you show me what you mean later."

"Woman, you know I love a challenge."

"Then consider yourself challenged."

After her "date" with Michael, Barbara sailed through the rest of her day, barely able to keep her feet on solid ground. She felt good inside, really good for the first time in ages. Once she'd finally let go of her doubts, it all felt right. Sure Michael was young. But he made her feel young, too. She felt alive again, and sexy and needed.

For so long after Marvin's passing, she'd literally turned herself off, devoting all of herself to her work and the few hours per week that she spent with her friends. There was a part of her that felt she was somehow betraying the memory of what she and Marvin had shared if she even so much as thought about getting involved with someone. As a result, she'd let herself go, gained some unwanted pounds, rarely went to the hair salon or had her nails and toes done. She figured, what was the point, there was no one in or out of her life that she wanted to impress.

But what Michael had brought into her world was a sense of value. She didn't want to be better for him, she wanted to do it for herself and he would simply be the very lucky beneficiary.

Before she left for the day, she made an appointment to get her hair done professionally the following day, and on the way home she stopped in the nail salon to have a manicure and pedicure. A woman had to start somewhere, she mused as the technician worked on her feet.

She sat back as the hot, sudsy water churned around her ankles. Yes, life was looking really good right about now. It truly was. Maybe she'd even sign up for the gym. She wanted to look just as good on the outside as she felt on the inside.

By the time she was done, it had begun to rain. Good thing she wasn't coming from the hair salon, she thought as she hurried toward her car parked on the next block. Before she'd reached the corner, the heavens opened and everyone was running for cover. She put her purse over her head, which was virtually useless and made a mad dash for the corner while she still had the light.

It was the last thing she remembered.

When she next opened her eyes, a bevy of strange, concerned faces hovered above her. Her head pounded, exacerbated by the bright light that was shining in her eyes.

"Ms. Allen, can you hear me?"

Barbara blinked in slow motion so as not to set off the rockets in her head. "Yes," she said, her voice sounding strange to her ears.

"You were in an accident. You're in the hospital in the emergency room. I'm Dr. Clarke."

Accident…hospital? She swallowed.

"We're going to take you up for X-rays. You have a minor concussion, but there doesn't appear to be any broken bones. You're a very lucky lady."

She didn't feel very lucky, but she supposed under the circumstances she was. What were the circumstances?

"What…happened?"

"You were hit by a car."

She flinched. Yes, now she remembered. She was crossing the street in the rain.

"Is there someone you want us to call—husband, family member?"

She had no husband and she was all that was left of her family. "Elizabeth…Lewis…my friend. Her number is in my cell phone."

The doctor murmured something to the nurse standing beside him. "We'll be sure she's notified. Now, let's get you up to X-ray. Make sure they do a full body scan and a head CT," Dr. Clarke said before walking out.

Hours later and after her X-ray and CAT scan, she was admitted for observation and put in a semiprivate room. Her headache had been reduced to a dull, pounding throb. Painful but at least it was bearable. Gingerly she turned her head to take in her surroundings: a typical hospital room, small, sterile and without ambience. A woman was in the next bed connected to a series of frightening-looking tubes, and the constant beep from the monitor was a chilling reminder of the fragility of life.

She closed her eyes and said a silent prayer. Although the doctor had not been back to see her, she was confident that she would be fine. God brought her too far, and too close to happiness to snatch it away now.

Barbara wasn't sure how long she'd slept, but when she awoke, Elizabeth was at her bedside, holding her hand. A slow smile crept across her mouth and Barbara could see that Elizabeth had been crying.

"I came as soon as they called me. Oh God, I'm so glad you're all right. I didn't know what to think."

"Thanks for coming, Ellie."

"You know I'm here for you, girl. How are you feeling?"

"Like I went headfirst into a brick wall at full speed."

Elizabeth winced. "Did they give you anything for the pain? Should I call someone?"

"They put something in the intravenous. It's helping a little."

Elizabeth let out a breath and pulled her chair closer to the bed. "Do you know what happened?"

"Not really. The last thing I remember was crossing the street in all that rain."

"Where were you?"

Barbara chuckled lightly and bombs exploded in

her head. She squeezed her eyes shut until the pain subsided to a bearable level. Slowly she opened her eyes. "The nail salon of all places. When was the last time I was there? And the first time I do, something like this happens. Life is a bitch, as they say."

"You got that right. But, honey, it could have been so much worse. I don't even want to think about it."

"Neither do I." Her eyes widened. "Michael!"

"What about him?"

"I need to call him."

"Give me his number. I'll call him and let him know what happened."

"He was supposed to be going out of town today for a few days. He may have left already." She waved her hand. "Don't bother him. I don't want him to be so far away and worried about me."

"Don't you think he'll worry even more if he calls and can't reach you?"

Barbara was thoughtful for a moment. "I guess you're right."

"Where's his number?"

"In my cell phone. Hopefully, my purse is in that drawer." She pointed to the table next to her bed.

Elizabeth looked inside and pulled out her purse. She took out the cell phone. "I can't use this in here."

"Oh, right. Okay, well, call him. Make sure you let him know that I am fine, Ellie, fine. And that I'll call him as soon as they let me out of here."

"Do you know when? Have they told you?"

"They haven't told me anything." She frowned for a moment, not wanting to become too concerned. The doctor hadn't been back to see her and if they admitted her, they must think that something is wrong, something they saw in the X-ray.

"Are you okay? You actually looked pale for a moment."

"Fine. I'm fine." She forced a smile. "Call Michael."

Elizabeth looked at her for a moment, trying to read the strained look on Barbara's face. "I'll be right back," she said and walked out of the room.

While Elizabeth was gone, Barbara ran over all the possibilities. She had no broken bones. Other than her head pounding, she didn't feel as if there was anything else wrong. Her body ached, and she was pretty sure it would get worse before it got better, but that was about it. Maybe it was no more than what the nurse said, they wanted to keep her for observation, as a precaution, nothing more, nothing less.

She folded her hands across her stomach and closed her eyes. In an instant your life could take such dramatic turns. One minute you were as happy and carefree as a kid on summer vacation, and the next… Well, it's like Ellie said, it could have been so much worse. Michael… She suddenly wished he was there with her. He had a way of making her feel so utterly comfortable and confident. She wanted to hear his voice, see his eyes when he told her that everything was going to be fine. Girl, you are getting it bad and that ain't good. She smiled, then, feeling a presence, she opened her eyes expecting to see Elizabeth.

Dr. Clarke walked in carrying a chart beneath his arm. He stepped up to her bed and drew the drapes.

Barbara's heart started racing and the pounding in her head kicked up another notch.

Dr. Clarke sat down. "I want to go over our findings."

Barbara swallowed.

"The head CT came back as I thought. You have a concussion, there's a small clot on the back of her head and your right temple seemed to take the brunt of the fall. You will be having some severe headaches for a while, possibly some light-headedness. They may even make you nauseous. But we'll give you medication to help with all that." He cleared his throat and Barbara braced herself for the other shoe to fall.

"During the body scan we noticed a small mass in your left breast."

Bile rose to her throat and set it on fire.

"When was the last time you had a mammogram?"

What was he asking her? She couldn't think. Small mass in her breast...

"Ms. Allen?"

Barbara blinked him back into focus. "I...last year."

He nodded. "Well, I've scheduled one for you first thing tomorrow morning. Depending on the results we will decide what to do there. If anything appears irregular, well, we will do an immediate biopsy to test the tissue." He turned the chart around to face her and pulled a pen from his smock pocket. "This is a consent form allowing us to perform the procedure."

Wait, this was going too fast. She was here for a bump on the head, a random accident, not to be told that she has a mass on her breast and a biopsy may be needed. What was he saying? How did one dot connect to the other? It didn't make sense.

"Ms. Allen, do you understand what I've explained to you?" His tone was one used on a small child or a dim-witted adult.

"No. I don't understand." She wouldn't cry. She wouldn't. She took deep breaths.

Dr. Clarke slowly repeated his findings, explaining in as much detail as he could what the procedure would be should the need arise.

"It could very well be nothing, Ms. Allen. But we want to be sure. You need to be sure."

Numb, she nodded her head.

"I'll leave the consent form with you and have the nurse pick it up later."

She nodded again.

He patted her shoulder. "Try to get some rest." He turned and walked out, nearly colliding with Elizabeth.

"Was that your doctor? What did he say?" She leaned toward the drawer and returned Barbara's cell phone to her purse. She stood and that's when she saw pure terror in Barbara's eyes. She grabbed her hand. "Hon, Barbara, what happened, what did he say?"

Barbara drew in a shuddering breath and in the next, tears streamed down her cheeks. After several false starts she was finally able to get it out.

For a moment, Elizabeth was stunned into silence. This was definitely not the time to say the first thing that came to mind, nor was it a time to spew a bunch of clichés. If nothing else, Barbara was pragmatic and Elizabeth knew that she wouldn't easily fall for soothing words that were meaningless—at least for now.

She took her hand. "I love you. And we'll wait together to find out the results and deal with it then."

Barbara nodded and offered a tight smile. "Don't tell Michael or the girls."

"I can hold off on the girls, but it's too late for Michael. When I told him what happened, he said he was catching the next plane out and he'd be here as soon as it landed."

Barbara squeezed her eyes shut. "I didn't think he would come. He just went back for training tryouts."

"That man is crazy about you, girl. If he could have found a way to come through the phone, I think he would have."

Barbara looked up at her friend. "I didn't think he really felt so strongly."

"That's part of your problem, my friend. You're always so busy caring about everyone else you never take time to enjoy all the people who really care about you."

She sniffed back more tears.

A nurse peeked her head in the door. "I'm sorry, but visiting hours are over."

Elizabeth nodded. She turned to Barbara. "I'll be here first thing in the morning."

"Okay," she whispered.

"Get some rest and think positive thoughts."

Barbara nodded. "Thanks, Ellie."

"For what, being your friend?"

Barbara smiled for real. "Yeah, for being my friend."

Elizabeth leaned down and kissed her on the forehead. "See you in the morning." She walked out.

Alone now, Barbara's mind ran the gamut of possibilities. She took the chart from the nightstand and slowly read the consent form. Finally she signed and set it back on the stand.

She said a long, silent prayer that no matter what happened, she would get through it with the love and support of her friends and Michael. She had things to do, an exciting life ahead of her, and she was going to live it to the fullest.

With that thought and powers greater than herself watching over her, she drifted off into a peaceful sleep.

Chapter 21

Elizabeth knew she shouldn't have done it without Barbara's permission, especially after she specifically asked her not to say anything, but she couldn't help herself. Besides, it was only right.

She pulled up in front of Stephanie's building. Stephanie was waiting outside. She came over to the car.

"I already called my job and told them I wouldn't be in today and maybe not tomorrow, either. I'll follow you over to Ann Marie's."

"Okay." Elizabeth waited for Stephanie to get settled in her car before she pulled out.

Moments later they cruised to a stop in front of Ann Marie's building.

"Did you talk to her this morning? Is she okay?" Elizabeth asked.

"I haven't spoken to her since last night at the hospital. She said they wanted to do the procedure first thing this morning if need be," Ann Marie said.

"Well, let's just hope there's no need be."

Ann Marie marched over to her car and the three-woman brigade headed for the hospital.

After jockeying for a space in the hospital parking lot, the trio entered St. Luke's Hospital.

"Why did they bring she 'ere?" Ann Marie asked once they were inside. "Should 'ave taken 'er to NYU where she work." Her accent was in full effect.

"It was the closest hospital to where the accident took place," Elizabeth said.

Stephanie shook her head as they approached the information desk. "Damn with the other news, I almost forgot all about the car accident. Did they get the person who hit her?"

"Apparently he stayed around and waited for the ambulance and the police, thank goodness."

Ann Marie sucked her teeth. "Damn fool should 'ave him license revoke!"

"Too many crazy nondrivin' assholes on the road," Stephanie fumed.

"All that's true, but if this accident didn't happen, Barb may have not known anything about the lump until…" Her words drifted off, but they got her meaning. She was the first one at the information desk.

"We're here to see Barbara Allen. She was brought in yesterday."

The receptionist did a search on the computer then

opened a file and pulled out three passes and handed them to Elizabeth. "Take the elevator to your left."

"Thanks." Elizabeth handed a pass to each woman.

Even though they were the only ones on the elevator there was total silence between them, each caught in her private thoughts.

The door opened on the sixth floor.

"Her room is down the hall," Elizabeth said, leading the way.

When they entered, Barbara's bed was empty and a unified gasp rippled through them.

Michael stood.

"They had to do the biopsy," he said.

Ann Marie, Stephanie and Elizabeth seemed to lose the starch in their spines.

"I'm Michael." He stepped closer. "You must be Ann Marie, Elizabeth…Stephanie." He shook each of their hands.

"I'm so glad you came. And I know Barbara will be, too," Elizabeth said.

"Did you get to see her?" Stephanie asked.

"For a few minutes. She was…Barbara." He smiled.

Ann Marie stepped up, dwarfed by his height. "Did they say how long?" She craned her neck to look at him.

"At least another half hour. The nurse came in a few minutes ago to let me know that they'd taken her up to surgery."

"Barbara told us so much about you," Ann Marie said.

"Did she?" He grinned, flashing sparkling even teeth. "She told me all about you ladies, as well. That's how I knew just who was who."

Elizabeth eased Ann Marie out of the way as she saw Ann's predatory claws flexing.

"When did you get in?"

"About six this morning." He jerked his head toward his bag near the bed. "I came straight from the airport."

"Barbara is a lucky lady," Stephanie said.

"I'm the lucky one."

The duty nurse stepped in. "She's in recovery. They should be bringing her back to her room shortly."

"Thank you," they said in unison.

Elizabeth, always the mother, went to Barbara's bed and began straightening the sheets. "Can't have her coming back to a messy room."

"She needs flowers, some ambience," Ann Marie said. "I'm going to run down to the gift shop." She darted out, her high heels clicking against the linoleum floor.

"Getting your hair done always makes you feel better." Stephanie opened up her oversize bag and pulled out her curling iron, comb, brush, hair oil and a silk scarf.

Just then, Dawne and Desiree came rushing in.

"We closed the shop so we could be here," Dawne said as soon as her booted foot crossed the threshold.

"How's Auntie?" Desiree asked.

"She should be coming back any minute now," Elizabeth said, kissing one daughter and then the next. "These are my daughters," she said, turning to Michael. She introduced Dawne then Desiree.

"Nice to meet you."

"You must be Michael," they said in perfect sync.

He chuckled. "Yes, I am."

"Go, Auntie," Desiree murmured. Dawne nudged her in the ribs. "Ouch!"

Michael angled his head to the right. "You called Barbara aunt."

"She's our godmother," Desiree offered. "Calling Aunt Barb 'Godmother' sounded so... 'Godfather,' ya know." She grinned.

Michael laughed.

Just then an orderly and a nurse wheeled Barbara to the room door. The tiny space, overflowing with well-wishing friends, was a welcome sight to Barbara. Everyone moved left, right, back and front to make room. The nurse and orderly lifted Barbara from the rolling bed onto her own.

She looked around at all the anxious faces and such a warm feeling began to fill her, replacing the dark cold abyss that had settled in her center since the day before.

"You'll all be happy to know that I'm fine. The mass was benign. They took it out and I can go home tomorrow or the day after."

A cheer went up in the room like being witness to the winning shot in the final seconds of a basketball game.

"Thank God!" Elizabeth said just as Ann Marie returned with the flowers.

"From the look on everyone's faces it must be good news!" The bouquet of flowers was nearly bigger than the bearer.

"Yes, it is," Stephanie said, and did a little dance that tickled Desiree and Dawne to no end.

Michael came forward and took the flowers from Ann Marie before she toppled over and put them on the bedside table.

"Thanks, Annie, they're beautiful." Barbara looked up at Michael. "You didn't have to come."

"Yes, I did. And I'm not leaving your side until I know you are one hundred and fifty percent."

"But what about your training, the coach, the new season? You've worked so hard to get back, Mike—"

He put his finger to her lips. "Enough. Quiet as it's kept, Ms. Allen, I'm a big boy and can make my own decisions."

"But—"

"No buts. I'm staying and that's it."

"Ooooow, someone who can put Aunt Barb in

check," Desiree teased. "I like him, Aunt Barb."
She winked.

"You like every cute guy you see," Dawne said.

Desiree made a face.

"Well, now that we know you're going to be okay,
why don't we give you and Michael some breathing
room," Elizabeth said, putting her arms around the
waists of her daughters then looking from Stephanie
to Ann Marie.

"Excellent idea," Stephanie said. "I'll do your hair
when you get home." She gathered up her supplies.

"I'll fix you a big pot of chicken soup when you
come home," Ann Marie said.

"Thank you, everyone, for coming, for everything." She held her cheek up for the parade of kisses.

One by one they left, leaving her and Michael alone.

"You have some great friends," he said, pulling up
a chair next to the bed.

"Yeah, I do," she said, appreciating them in a way
she hadn't before.

In the years they'd all been friends, she'd simply
accepted them as her girls, friends to hang out with,
share food, a movie and a personal story here and
there. But something had changed between them,
evolved and grown. Perhaps the change was a result
of the night they finally removed the veils that
shielded so many parts of themselves. And now, as
they were ready to embark on a new journey of

friendship and trust with their daring venture, what they'd built together over the years would be raised to another level and truly tested. She was looking forward to it, especially now that she had a new lease on life. She intended to live it to the fullest.

She glanced into Michael's warm, concerned eyes. Yeah, she was going to live it up. She couldn't wait to get home.

Chapter 22

Ann Marie turned the key in the lock and opened the door to her apartment. A sharp gasp caught in her throat. Phil and Raquel turned in her direction.

Phil stood up slowly, his gaze never leaving hers.

Ann Marie pulled herself together in the blink of an eye. She stretched her mouth into a smile, praying that it would hide the turmoil she felt inside.

"Baby, what you doing 'ere?" She rushed over to him, wrapped her arms around him and kissed him on the mouth. He was about as yielding as an oak tree. Ann Marie stepped back. Her eyes darted in Raquel's direction.

"I thought I'd surprise you." His jaw clenched.

Ann Marie's laugh was more of a hiccup. "I'm glad you're 'ere."

"Are you?" He looked at her for a long, tense moment. "We need to talk, Annie."

Ann Marie jutted her chin. "Fine. Let me get out of these clothes." She hurried out of the room before she got sick. This was not how she'd planned to tell Phil about Raquel. Her hope had been to get Raquel out of her house before Phil returned from the coast. Raquel being there had surely screwed up her life, big-time. How in the hell would she be able to explain to Phil? Worse what had Raquel told him?

Her fingers shook as she tried to unfasten the buttons on her shirt. What was she going to do? She blew out a ragged breath. She'd never seen Phil look at her with anything but lust and admiration in his eyes. What she saw in them today was disappointment, maybe even disgust.

She pulled off her blouse and tossed it on the bed. She'd just explain, that's all. She'd simply tell him… What?

Ann Marie went to the closet, pulled out a pair of soft gray sweatpants and a T-shirt. She took her time getting dressed, delaying the inevitable. When there was nothing left to do, no more stall tactics, she opened the bedroom door and walked out to face her accusers.

When she reentered the living room only Phil was present. At least she wouldn't have to deal with both of them.

"Hey, baby, sorry I took so long." She hurried over to him and sat on his lap, leaning close for a kiss. He turned his head, lifted her up and sat her next to him.

"Not now, Ann."

He may as well have slapped her. She blinked

back her surprise. She'd never before failed to get on his good side with offers of physical pleasure.

"Why, Ann, why did you feel it necessary not to tell me about…your daughter?"

She looked away, searching the room for the words that she hoped were hiding somewhere.

"I thought we had something."

"We do." She reached out to stroke his cheek. He pushed her hand away. Slowly she put her hand in her lap. "Fine, if this is the way you're going to be there's no point in trying to talk to you."

"Don't put this off on me. You were the one that lied."

She sprang up from her seat, hands on hips. "I never lied to you."

"Intentionally omitting the truth is a close cousin to lying."

She jerked her chin forward. "Raquel has nothing to do with us."

"She's a part of you. Of course she has something to do with us! What did you think I was going to do if you told me—run? Do you think so little of me?"

"No," she murmured. "Of course not."

"Then why?"

Why? It was a damn good question. One she'd asked herself more times than she could count. Raquel was a reflection of all the things Ann Marie was not. When she looked at Raquel she reminded

Ann Marie of her motherhood, of her vulnerability, of her inability to nurture, to provide, to support and show love. She reflected all her faults and she couldn't bear to look at what she saw, to be reminded, because then she would be forced to deal with it.

"I'm not going to explain myself. I have a daughter. Now you know." She shrugged in nonchalant fashion. "What else is there to say?"

"I don't know who you are," he said, his voice laden with disappointment. "And that scares me." He shook his head. "If you could so easily keep this from me, I don't even want to imagine what else you'd lie about or try to hide." He reached for his jacket, which he'd tossed on the couch. "And I don't want to find out."

He brushed past her and walked to the door, his footsteps sounding like bombs in Ann Marie's ears. She wanted to blurt it all out: her hurt, confusion, her fears. She wanted to tell him how desperately she wanted to be a real mother to her child but she didn't know how. So she watched him walk out the door and out of her life.

She drew in a long deep breath as the door shut behind him. It was best this way.

She turned away from the door. Raquel stood there.

"I didn't mean to mess up anything for you, Mama. He asked who I was. I told him."

Ann Marie waved off her comment.

"Am I a secret, Mama?"

What could she say? How could she tell her that the only people in the world who knew about her were Elizabeth, Barbara and Stephanie?

"No…I just never told Phil."

"Why? Do you think that by not talking about me it would make me disappear?"

"Why are you really here, Raquel? You have a husband and a life. So you had a little spat. That's no reason to walk out of your marriage." She pursed her lips in frustration.

"You've finally decided to ask me?" Her laugh was sad and filled with pain. Raquel sighed. "He left me."

"He'll come back. They always do. Let him get it out of his system. You don't let some other woman take your man." She thought of Elizabeth and her crumbled marriage, but it was still good advice. She would have told Elizabeth the same thing if she hadn't been so teary-eyed and hysterical.

"He didn't leave me for another woman."

"What? What are you saying?" Her pulse rate rose by degrees.

"He left me for a man."

All the air whooshed out of Ann Marie's body. In slow motion she moved toward the couch, reached out her hand to brace herself and sat down. She looked up at her daughter. "How do you know? Are you sure?"

Raquel walked around the armchair and sat. "He told me." She folded her hands in her lap.

Now she really felt sick. Her mind raced to an ugly possibility. "Have you been tested?"

Raquel shook her head no. "I'm so scared, Mama." She looked at her mother as tears slid down her cheeks.

Ann Marie was paralyzed. She stared at her daughter as Raquel silently begged for her comfort.

From a place she didn't know existed within her she felt a surge of compassion that took her from her seat to her daughter's side. Without thought, her arms went around her daughter and drew her close. Suddenly, Raquel was no longer a grown woman out on her own, but the tiny baby she'd held and looked at in awe so many years ago. The baby who needed her for her survival. Ann Marie rocked her baby in her arms, stroked her hair, gently shushed her sobs.

"It's going to be all right, baby. It will." She rocked her some more. Her thoughts were so scattered. She didn't want to imagine the worst. She held her daughter tighter. It was going to be fine. It had to be.

Chapter 23

"Here's your pill," Michael said, handing her the pain medicine and a glass of water.

"You've really got to stop fussing over me," Barbara said, secretly tickled by all of Michael's attention. She took the pill and washed it down with water. "Ever since I got home you've been waiting on me hand and foot. I'm really okay, you know."

He sat down on the side of her bed. "I decided that when I got the news about the accident and then the surgery that I wasn't going to waste one more moment of not giving you my all. Life is too short, precious. Besides, don't you think it's time someone took care of you for a change?"

She took his hand. "You know how much I appreciate everything, don't you?"

"Sure."

"But...I can't help but feel guilty that you've put your life and possibly your career on the line for me."

"Careers come and go, Barb. I could go out on that

court, get hurt and be a cripple for the rest of my life. They could decide to bench me for the season, anything could happen. Besides, it's time I started looking at life beyond the next jump shot. I want to start thinking about the future, a real future for me... for us."

Her heart banged in her chest. "What are you saying?"

He grinned. "Don't look so panicked. All I'm saying, for now, is that I want us to see where this relationship is going to take us. I want to be with you, be a real part of your life and you a part of mine. Is that cool with you?"

She smiled. The tension eased in her stomach. "It's cool."

"Good." He stood. "Ready for lunch?"

She laughed. "Yes, but only if you let me help you fix it...for both of us."

"On one condition."

"What?" Her eyes widened.

Suddenly he bent down and scooped her up into his arms. "If you let me carry you, right next to my heart." He pulled her close and kissed her long and slow.

Barbara's heart swelled with joy as warmth spread through her body. How long had it been that she'd felt so utterly special, so cared for and cared about? Elizabeth was right. It was way past time that she allowed someone to take care of her. And so far, Michael was doing a damn good job.

Stephanie hit a few keys on her computer, preparing a release for her new client, when Conrad walked in unannounced and without knocking.

She looked up, frowned. "The door is there for a reason."

He chuckled. "Having a bad day?"

"Not at all, but I'd prefer not to be disturbed. I'm busy."

He ignored her and crossed the room, picking up an award that sat on her desk then putting it back down.

"You've been avoiding me."

"Not now, Conrad."

"I miss you. Doesn't that count for anything?"

She stopped typing and pursed her lips. "What is it supposed to count for?"

"You're being really difficult, Stephanie. I don't like it when you're difficult."

"Look, Conrad…I can't do this anymore."

His expression hardened. "Do what?"

"This. This whatever this is between us." She swallowed. "It's over, done, I'm through."

"I put you in this office. I gave you your big break, made sure you had the high-priced clients, the commissions. And you say you're through." His laugh was nasty. "You're done when I say so." He jabbed a finger at his chest. "Me, not you. Got it?" He stared at her for a long moment then swept her award off the desk with the back of his hand, sending it sailing across the room. "Be home tonight. Don't make me use my key." He walked out and slammed the door behind him.

Stephanie covered her face with her hands. Her whole body trembled. She couldn't do this anymore. She couldn't let him touch her again. Ever. Then the image of her sister sitting in her room flashed in her head.

She could no longer let guilt hold her place. It had held her captive for more than a decade. She reached into her desk drawer and began pulling out files. Samantha, in her own way, knew that Stephanie loved her, even if she was unable to express it. And she could love her just as well in a place that she could afford. She had money saved and even after she made her contribution to the business, she would be okay for a little while.

Stephanie slipped a CD in the hard drive of her computer and began downloading files. A little more than a half hour later she was done.

She went into the supply room and got a box. Returning to her office, she packed her awards, files and her treasured Rolodex. She added the CDs then sealed up the box.

With determination beneath each footstep, she went to Conrad's office and without knocking went inside.

Conrad smiled. "Changed your mind early?" Then he noticed the box and that she had on her coat. "What's with the box?"

"I'm leaving."

He shrugged. "Early day. Good, then you have plenty of time to get ready for me."

"No. You don't get it. I quit."

He looked at her for a moment then started laughing. "You're kidding. You can't quit. What would you do?"

"I'll figure it out."

"Don't be a fool. I'll see to it that you never get another job in this town."

"Do whatever you want, Conrad. Frankly, my dear, I don't give a damn."

With that, she walked out and she'd never felt so free.

Chapter 24

Barbara had been home from the hospital for three weeks and her doctor determined that it was fine for her to return to work. She'd gotten used to Michael being with her during the days and loving her up at night. To be truthful, she was getting used to this new life.

Michael looked at her from across the table. "My coach called yesterday evening."

Barbara picked up her glass of orange juice and took a sip. "And?"

"He told me if I wasn't back in Miami by next Monday, I'd be cut from the team."

"Then you have to go back." She set her glass down. "You are going back, aren't you?"

"I've been thinking about it."

"And?"

"I don't want to leave you here."

"I'm fine. I'm going back to work on Monday. I can't let you screw up your career. Go back. I'll be here when training is over."

"Will you?" He pushed up from the table and went to the sink.

"What are you saying?"

"If I go back and get through training, once the season starts I'll be traveling at least six months out of the year. When I'm not playing, or on a plane, I'm practicing. And when I'm not doing any of that, I'm beat." He turned toward Barbara. "There won't be any time for us. And we're just getting started."

"Mike, I'm not a little girl that needs to be constantly entertained. I have plenty to keep me busy. And with the mortgage being approved for the house, I'm going to have my hands full, as well."

He leaned against the sink. "So where does that leave us?"

"It leaves us like a lot of couples—we work it out."

He lowered his head a moment, chuckled lightly then looked up at her. "One thing I've learned in being with you on a daily basis is that you like familiarity, you like security, knowing how things are going to be. If I go back out on the road, that's out of the question."

Barbara got up from the table and came to him. She put her arms around his waist and rested her head on his chest.

"If it's meant to work it will," she said softly. "What we have is good, it's wonderful, more than I

could have ever expected." She stepped back and
looked up at him. "But as you said, I'm pragmatic,
but also very realistic. You have a life, a career, and
so do I. And both of us have to go on about the
business of life. You care about me because of who
I am and I'm attracted to you because of who you are.
You want to give up something you love for someone
you've known less than a year. I don't want you to
look back and regret it and resent me."

"I hate it when you make sense." He smiled. "It
could be so easy to just be with you."

"And boring. I'd give you another week and you'd
be ready for restraints." She paused a moment. "Go
back. Do what you need to do. Don't use us as a
reason not to see if you still have what it takes."

He pulled her close. "You're the perfect reason to
come back home, something to look forward to at the
end of the road."

"I like the sound of that…having something to
look forward to."

He slid his hands in between the folds of her robe
and ran his fingers along the smooth surface of her
back. She closed her eyes and sighed. He pressed
against her.

"It's been awhile," he whispered in her ear.

"Too long," she said, arching her back and lifting
her pelvis to meet the slow undulations of his hips.

Michael pushed the robe off her shoulders, draw-

ing in a deep breath as he looked at her. With a tenderness that made her cry out, he cupped her breasts,
stroking the nipples until they rose and hardened
beneath his fingertips. Barbara whimpered. His
fingers grazed over the small scar from the incision
beneath her right breast and they both silently gave
a sigh of thanks. He unfastened the belt of Barbara's
robe and it fell to the floor.

"We've never done it on the kitchen table," he
said with a wicked look in his eyes.

Barbara giggled. "Wanna try?"

"Absolutely." His hand reached between her legs.
"Remember that scene with Jack Nicholson in *The
Postman Always Rings Twice?*" He ran hot kisses
along her neck as he eased her across the room, fin-
gering her ever so gently. "When he took Jessica
Lange right on the kitchen table?"

Her body pulsed. "Yes." The backs of her thighs
brushed up against the table an instant before he
lifted her and set her atop the smooth surface.

He spread her thighs. "So do I."

"I'll call you as soon as I land," Michael said when
they pulled up at Kennedy Airport.

"Make sure that you do." Barbara cupped his chin
in her palm and pulled him toward her for a long slow
kiss. Her tongue danced and teased his, committing
the feel and taste to memory. He'd be gone for a

month if everything worked out—a long time. She'd gotten used to his loving, morning, noon and night and any other time they could squeeze in. She'd come to expect it. She loved the security of knowing that he was there when she got up in the morning and then at the end of the day. It was almost like…being married again.

She eased away before foolish thoughts got the best of her. "You're going to miss your plane," she said against his mouth.

He took a deep breath and searched her eyes. "I'll call you."

She nodded. "Go, go."

He got out then grabbed his bag from the back seat. "Drive safe," he said.

"I will."

He waved then turned and walked through the revolving doors into the terminal. Within moments he was swallowed up in the crowd and in that instant Barbara realized how much her life had changed. She'd grown complacent and "settled" in her life as a widow, with a job she enjoyed and was comfortable with. Then in a blink her life had taken on new dimensions, a new turn, the world was exciting again.

"You're gonna have to move that car, ma'am," an officer said, tapping on her window.

Barbara blinked, looked up. "Oh…sorry." Slowly she pulled out into the exiting traffic.

As she merged with the cars, watching the signs and the scenery change, the lanes open, drivers and passengers eager to get to their destinations, she understood that the doors to her new life had fully opened. All she had to do was step across that threshold and explore all the possibilities.

Tonight would be the first night in weeks that she'd spent without Michael and a perfect time to have a girls' night and catch up with her friends' lives and make some plans for the house. The closing was in a week and after that it would be full steam ahead again.

A surge of excitement raced through her, giving her a shiver of anticipation. As soon as she got home, she'd give the ladies a call, whip up a menu and plan for a fun evening.

She turned on the radio and wouldn't you know it, Chaka was belting out, "I'm Every Woman." Barbara tossed her head back and laughed, tapped her fingers against the steering wheel and sang along with her. "Yeah, Chaka, *it's all in me!*"

Chapter 25

Barbara checked and rechecked her apartment. Everything was spic and span. If she concentrated really hard she could still smell Michael's scent in the air. She wondered if the girls would be able to, also.

She smiled as she set some snacks out on her grandmother's table. Michael had called twice since he'd arrived in Miami, once when he landed and then when he reached his hotel. He'd promised to check on her in the morning once Barbara told him about the girls' night. He'd laughed, telling her that he wished he could be there for the catch-up session, and wished her luck on the plans for the house.

Barbara hummed along with Regina Bell's "If I Could," as she set out the dip and filled the ice bucket. Thank goodness she was off all her medication. She could sure use a drink, and what better way to break back into the game but with her girls.

As usual, Ann Marie arrived first, followed by Elizabeth then Stephanie.

Everyone was talking and laughing at once as they dropped off their contributions for dinner.

"So where's Mr. Young and Handsome?" Stephanie asked as she filled her small paper plate with shrimp cocktail then popped one in her mouth.

Barbara sat back and smiled, the kind of smile a woman has when she is totally satisfied. "He's in Miami. Went back for training and to see if that knee is going to hold up for the new season."

"I'm sure you've been giving it a good workout," Ann Marie said.

"I try not to hurt the young boy." Barbara laughed and the girls joined in.

"See what a little young lovin' can do for ya," Stephanie said, and winked at Barbara. "I quit my job," she said in the next breath.

The trio looked in her direction.

"You did?" Elizabeth asked. "What did Conrad say?"

"Blew a fuse, but I don't care and I told him as much. He said he'd make sure I never got another job in New York."

"Can he really do that?" Barbara asked.

Stephanie shrugged. "Probably."

"Why don't you file a sexual harassment suit against him?" Barbara said.

Stephanie slowly shook her head, no. "They'd never

believe me. And I'd probably only make bad matters worst. I want to put it behind me and move on."

"So what are you going to do for money?" Ann Marie asked.

Stephanie flashed a look in her direction, trying to figure out if the question was borne of concern or another one of her digs.

"I have money saved. I'll be all right." She looked at Ann Marie. "Thanks for asking."

"Steph, you are totally talented," Barbara said. "You'll be fine. Maybe it's about time you started thinking about...doing your own thing."

"Actually, I have been." She looked from one face to the other. "And I thought that my first project would be a full-out Pause for Men campaign, with all the bells and whistles."

"Ooow, do you mean we might be famous? On TV, maybe *Oprah?*" Elizabeth squeaked, clapping her hands.

Stephanie laughed. "One thing I've learned as a publicist—" she wagged her finger "—never promise your clients fame, just that you'll make them look as good as you possibly can and put their name and brand in front of every face that matters."

"If anyone can do it, Stephanie can," Ann Marie said, surprising everyone, but no one more than Stephanie.

"Do you really mean that?" Stephanie asked with a mixture of disbelief and awe.

Ann Marie reached across the table and took Stephanie's hand. "Yes, I really mean it."

Stephanie felt something give way inside, and the dam that she'd kept plugged up for so long burst open. Between tears she spilled out the whole story of her sister, Samantha, trapped in a body that refused to obey, a mind confined in some unreachable place. Her friends comforted her, made her smile, stiffened her spine and poured their faith into her.

"You're who we need to put Pause for Men on the map," Elizabeth said. "You start with us, and get bigger and bigger clients. You'll be able to take care of Samantha."

Stephanie sniffed hard and wiped her eyes and nose with a napkin that Ann Marie handed her. "And there's no time like the present," Ann Marie said. "Got your laptop?"

Stephanie nodded. "I don't leave home without it," she said, her smile growing stronger.

"So...let's see what you have in that PR whiz head of yours," Barbara said, pulling up her chair to her grandmother's table.

Stephanie opened up her laptop and showed them the PR plan that she'd been working on since she'd walked out of her job. She stole a glance at Ann Marie, the one least likely to support her, and received a smile of encouragement as she explained the time-table. Maybe Ann Marie wasn't such a bitch after all.

By the time the ladies left, it was well after midnight. But Barbara wasn't in the least bit tired. Rather, she felt energized. Within the next few weeks renovations on the building would begin. They were planning to start with the roof, then the top floor. Elizabeth announced that she was selling her house and that she would move into the brownstone as a live-in caretaker as soon as the top-floor apartment was ready. It's the perfect way to start my new life, she'd said without a hint of regret in her voice.

Barbara was happy for Elizabeth. For a while she was really concerned that she wouldn't be able to get beyond what Matthew had done. But she had. What stunned her more than anything was Ann Marie. In her own unique way she'd reached out and made her peace with Stephanie, and Steph had somehow found the courage to break free from Conrad.

She turned out the lights in the living room. Life was all about getting to the good part. She went into the bedroom, got undressed and slid beneath the cool sheets—her first night alone in some time. She reached for the phone next to the bed and dialed Michael's hotel room. A little late-night sweet talk was just what she needed.

Chapter 26

"You can't do this, Elizabeth," Matthew said, running his hand across his close-cut hair as he paced in front of her.

Elizabeth sat back in the kitchen chair with her arms folded and her right leg rocking leisurely across her left beneath the table. Whenever Matthew was nervous his top lip began to sweat. It was sweating now. She felt smug and oh so powerful.

"I can and I have. While you were so busy at work, you left everything up to me, remember? You may have been paying the mortgage all these years, but the house is in my name since you had such crappy credit when we were house hunting." She smiled. "Remember? I'm the sole owner of this half-million-dollar home."

Matthew stopped so short his shoes squeaked against the black-and-white linoleum.

She exhaled a satisfied sigh. "I guess it's coming back to you now."

Matthew glared at her. "You would sell the house right from under me?"

"You were ready to put me on the street," she said, her voice as even as a straight line. "I think it's only fair that I be duly compensated for the mental anguish, don't you, not to mention adultery?" She covered her mouth in mock alarm. "Oh, I did say not to mention the A word." Slowly she pushed up from her seat. "Who knows, I might feel generous and give you a settlement after the sale of the house—on one condition."

"What?"

"That you face your daughters and tell them yourself exactly why you left."

He lowered his head, and his body appeared to crumble. "I…can't face them."

She shrugged. "Fine. Then we have nothing else to discuss. I'll have my lawyer contact yours with all the proper amendments to the divorce. Our business is finished. Thanks for dropping by. You know your way out."

"This isn't like you, Ellie."

"I know, dear. There's a new sheriff in town. Now, if you'll excuse me, I have things to do." Gee, she wished she smoked. It would have been the perfect closing scene to light up.

Matthew slung his hands in his pockets. "Ellie—" he shook his head as he spoke, then looked at her

"—I'm sorry. I'm really sorry. You were...*are* a good wife and a great mother. I know you didn't deserve this."

The muscles in her throat tightened until she felt as if she would choke. When she looked at her husband now, right at this moment, he was the man she'd married. The handsome, loving, ambitious man who wanted nothing more in the world than to make her happy. Where had he gone? What had gone so terribly wrong that they'd arrived at this place?

She blinked back tears of regret and turned away from his searching eyes. "I really think you should go now, Matt."

"That's just it, Ellie, I don't want to go. I..."

Her gaze jumped in his direction right along with her racing heart. "What are you saying?"

"I'm saying that I made a mistake, a terrible, ugly mistake."

She gripped the edge of the table to keep from fainting. How many nights had she lain awake hoping, praying that this was all some silly misunderstanding, some miscommunication that happens in romance novels. And when the hero finally explains his side, the heroine melts and all is forgiven.

Hell, that was a romance novel. This was for real, her life, her feelings. There wasn't anything remotely fantasy filled about them.

"I'm sorry to hear that, Matthew."

"What?" He frowned in confusion.

"I'm sorry to hear that after all you've put me through, put your daughters through, you've suddenly awakened and realized that you made a mistake."

"I want to come back home, Ell." He took a step toward her.

Her nerves vibrated so violently she thought they'd ignite and singe her skin. She found the courage to look him in the eye. For a moment she wavered, remembering the good times, the loving, the children she'd carried, the times they'd shared. But what rested foremost on her mind was not the past but the present, the here and now. He'd taken them to a place of no return.

He reached out to her. "It could be good again, Ell. Better. I swear I'll make it up to you."

Her smile was sad and filled with longing and regret. "I can't." She turned her back to him. "Please leave, Matthew. Now."

"Ell…" His hand was on her shoulder. It burned to the marrow of her bones. He turned her around and pulled her close. "Please Ell."

She pressed her hands against his chest and slowly shook her head. "No, Matt. I can't do it. I won't."

His jaw rocked back and forth and his expression hardened by degrees. "Fine." He stepped away. "Have your lawyer call mine." He snatched up his jacket from the back of the kitchen chair and stormed out.

Elizabeth released a shuddering breath, holding on to the side of the table for support as she bent in half, drawing in large gulps of air.

Slowly she stood and miraculously she didn't feel even a hint of tears. She was going to be all right. She went to the fridge and took out a bottle of water, twisted the cap and took a nice cool swallow.

Wow, a half-million dollars was nothing to sneeze at. She might have begged to come back, too.

She finished off her water and tossed the empty bottle in the recycle bin. She looked around. She'd spent some of the best years of her life in this house, she thought as she moved from room to room. But it was only a building, not some spiritual entity. With her marriage all but a period, it would do her a world of good to start her new life in a new place.

She smiled, feeling very optimistic. She knew just how she wanted to fix up her new place…and she had the money to do it.

Chapter 27

"So you're really going to do it?" Michael said as he and Barbara sat opposite each other at Spoonbread Restaurant.

As usual for a weekend, the small, family-run soul-food restaurant was packed—surprisingly, with white couples and the yuppie students who dormed at Columbia University a few blocks away.

Barbara added a dash of hot sauce to her collard greens. "Yep. We closed on the building on Wednesday. Ann Marie is working out the details of the business license and the contractors that you recommended are coming by to give us an estimate on Monday." She brought him up to date with Stephanie and Elizabeth, leaving out the really sordid details. He'd surprised her by coming in for the weekend and she couldn't be happier.

He tore into a barbecue spare rib, savoring the rich, thick sauce. For a moment he closed his eyes in pure bliss. "Mmm, mmm, mmm, the food here is great! Make a man leave home in the middle of the night for these ribs."

Barbara laughed.

"That's one thing that Miami is lacking, good soul-food restaurants."

"More reason for you to spend time here."

He looked across the table at her. "I have my reason. You."

She blushed then focused on her greens.

"What are you going to do about your job?"

Barbara put her fork down and sighed thoughtfully. "Well, my plan is to work at the house part-time while we build the business. When it takes off then I'll leave."

Michael nodded. "Makes sense. You seem so focused and certain. Aren't you even a little bit scared?"

"You know, I thought I would be. But after seeing the place, talking with my friends and finally understanding that it's long past time for me to do something for Barbara, I said the hell with fear and just go for it."

"That's the only way to make any real change in your life is to take that leap of faith."

"Like you and me?"

"Yeah, just like you and me." He picked up his napkin and dabbed at a spot of potato salad from the corner of her mouth. "Come on, finish up. I want to show you how much you've been missed."

"Sounds like dessert to me." She put her knife and fork down and finished off her iced tea.

"Exactly."

"Hmm, my mouth is craving something sweet," she cooed.

The corner of his mouth curved upward. "So is mine, baby, so is mine."

As they walked hand in hand back to Barbara's apartment she thought about how much her life had changed, but more importantly how she had changed in the past few months.

When she was married to Marvin—God rest his soul—she never imagined herself as a sexual person or even sexy, for that matter. Prior to her marriage she'd been with one other man and that had ended in disaster of epic proportions. It was a lifetime ago. A time she'd shared with no one—not her friends, not even Marvin. Once she was a married woman, sex was simply sex, something married people did. Marvin wasn't the adventurous type. He frowned at X-rated movies, and sex toys or sex talk didn't enter into their marriage. You could hold a gun to his head and he wouldn't perform oral sex. It was simply taboo in his mind.

So, she simply accepted her sex life for what it was: a duty. More often than not, she didn't experience a climax, but she'd grown used to that, as well. She often wondered about her girlfriends, what their experiences were like, but she'd been so conditioned not to discuss the subject since she was a young girl that she couldn't fix her mouth to broach the topic—not even with her closest friend, Elizabeth. And although Stephanie and Ann Marie were in no way shy about relaying their escapades, she could never see herself reciprocating. For the most part she thought they must be lying. Sex could never be as mind-shattering as they'd said.

Ha, that's what she thought until she made love with Michael. Lawdhavemercy, just thinking about it got her panties all damp. The morning after was always filled with aches and pains, having used muscles she didn't know existed, but the getting there was well worth it.

"So what is your coach saying about the knee?" she asked, needing to get her mind out of his shorts for a minute.

"So far so good. They have me on a restricted training program. I still get therapy every day and he's letting me practice for longer periods of time. Our first scrimmage is next week. That'll be the real test."

"Mike?"

"Yes." He looked down at her.

"Have you ever considered—seriously considered what you would do if you couldn't ever play again? I mean, you're barely into your thirties."

"I've been thinking about that a lot lately. Espe-

cially since the accident and meeting you." He paused
a moment. "I have a good deal of money socked
away and some solid investments. I know I want to
remain in sports in some capacity. I'd been thinking
of opening a training camp for inner-city kids."

"Really?"

He nodded. The excitement lit his eyes in the
twilight. "For so many urban kids sports is a way out,
ya know. I mean, everyone won't be a star, but at least
it will provide them with an option."

"I think it's a great idea. Something sorely missing
and needed."

"Exactly. So…we'll see how things go with my
career and then I'll decide."

"Have you thought about where you want the
camp to be?"

"You're here, so what better place to start?"

For a reason that she couldn't quite grasp, his
answer unsettled her.

They reached her apartment building and she
pushed the thought aside. For now, only pleasure
would be on her mind.

Michael was right when he said he wanted to show
her how much he'd missed her. They made a game
of foreplay, moving from one room of the apartment
to the next as they stripped and played with each
other's bodies.

He loved to make love to her in the light and she'd grown comfortable with her body, proud of her womanly curves and that extra dip in her hips. She was no longer shy about looking at him fully erect and throbbing. It gave her a sense of her womanly powers that she could do that to him, time and again.

When they half stumbled, half laughed their way into the kitchen, Michael did something with an ice cube that should be illegal.

He emptied the ice tray into a plastic bowl and put it on the table.

Barbara's brown eyes widened. "What do you plan to do with that?"

Michael winked and crooked his finger, beckoning her to him. She crossed the cool tile floor, totally unselfconscious. Even the slight jiggle in her stomach didn't bother her.

"Yes, Mr. Townsend? What can I do for you?"

"It's more like what I'm going to do for you." He took a cube of ice from the bowl, sucked on it for a moment then used it to create a trail down the valley of her breasts. After the first startling feel of it, Barbara embraced the new sensation. He used another cube to circle her nipples, making them stand on end. She shuddered but not from the cold. Everywhere he stroked her with the ice he followed it with his mouth, his tongue licking up the droplets of water. Just when she thought she couldn't take much more, he took a cube of ice and slid it back and forth across her clit.

Her inner thighs trembled and she grabbed onto his shoulders to keep from falling to the floor.

"Michael," she gasped.

"Go with it, baby," he whispered in her ear an instant before he slipped the cube inside her.

Her climax was immediate and so intense she swore she blacked out for a moment. And still Michael wasn't done with her. While the explosions continued to erupt, he slid down until his mouth reached her center and sent her over the edge one more time.

She'd heard of "whip appeal" but she'd always associated it with a woman's sexual hold over a man. Barbara curled closer to the warmth of Michael's body. She was pretty sure that's what she was suffering from, and she had it bad. As much as she loved what Michael did for her and to her, the way he'd made her feel about herself awakened her sexuality, there was a part of her that knew she couldn't keep up with him—not for long, anyway.

He was barely thirty. By the time he was forty she'd be sixty. Menopause would have sealed her fate by then and a cube of ice she'd need more for hot flashes than turn-ons.

She pressed her lips against the curve of his spine and wrapped her arm around his narrow waist. Inch by inch her fingers traveled down his hard belly until she reached his partially erect penis. She took it in her hand and stroked him slow and steady, bringing him to full attention.

He groaned with delight and turned around to face her.

What the hell, she thought. You only live once.

Chapter 28

Elizabeth volunteered to meet the contractors at the house at 7:30 a.m. Ann Marie promised to come as soon as she was finished with a closing on another property, which probably wouldn't be until late afternoon. Stephanie had a policy of never leaving the house before nine, and Barbara would arrive as soon as she got off work at four.

When Elizabeth pulled up in front of the house, a guy who looked like he belonged on the cover of *Contractors 'R Us,* complete with faded jeans, weatherworn plaid shirt with sleeves rolled up, revealing muscled arms, stood in front of the house with the brim of his baseball cap pulled low over his eyes.

Something inside her jumped and shifted. She eased into an available parking space and got out, thankful that she'd put on some makeup and had her hair done over the weekend.

She stretched out her hand as she approached. "Hi, I'm Elizabeth Lewis, one of the owners."

"Ron Powers." He took her hand.

It was hard, firm. Her head felt a little light and her stomach was doing something funny. His face was all rugged angles, the color of roasted coffee nuts with the hint of dark stubble on his cheeks and chin. His eyes were a remarkable cinnamon brown with curly black lashes and thick brows.

"Pleasure," he said, releasing her hand then angling his head over his broad shoulder. "Nice place. Solid foundation." He turned back to look at her. "Ready to go in? I want to take a look around, make some notes before the guys get here."

"S-ure," she managed to sputter, wondering if the rest of the "guys" looked anything like this hunk of a man.

They started at the top and Ron did some measurements in comparison to the schematics of the house that he had in a folder. He pulled a pen out of his back pocket.

Hmm, didn't think there was room for anything in those pockets the way his jeans snuggly hugged his rear end and outlined those powerful thighs, Elizabeth mused. A thin film of perspiration ran across her hairline. Was it hot in here or was it her overactive imagination?

"The first thing we'll do is strip the roof and recover it," he said, suddenly turning toward her.

She blinked him back into focus. "O-kay."

He gave her a half smile. "Are you okay? You look a bit flushed."

It was times like this that Elizabeth resented her sandstone complexion. All of her emotions rose to the surface of her skin.

"Fine. Just a little anxious about the house."

He chuckled lightly. "You're in good hands. My team is one of the best in the city. I'd trust them with my mother's house."

"Good to know."

"Do you live in the neighborhood?"

"Yes, up on Morningside Drive and One Sixteen."

His dark eyes widened. "Really? We're practically neighbors. I'm on Amsterdam and One Nineteen." He leaned against the mantel, appraising her. "I'm surprised we haven't run into each other before."

"I drive a lot," she said, and realized how silly that sounded.

He grinned. "You're in great shape for someone who drives all the time."

She didn't know what to say about that and felt as if she should hold her stomach in. Thank heavens for well-tailored designer sportswear. She couldn't remember the last time she'd had a conversation with a man who complimented her, other than her husband. "Thank you. I think."

Ron laughed a deep, soulful laugh that made her

smile in return. "You're quite welcome and yes, it was a compliment."

The floor didn't open up, so she had no other choice but to stand there and feel utterly ridiculous and quite naked under his exploring gaze. She tugged the opening of her sweat jacket closed. "So, uh, after you finish the roof, the first thing we want completed is the top floor."

"Right. It's on my list. But before we can do that I want to do a full assessment of the plumbing and electrical system. Ann Marie mentioned that she had some concerns because of the leaks, and the electricity must be brought up to code. You don't want to blow the whole house out every time you turn on the microwave."

"How long do you think your assessment will take?"

"Hmm…" He gazed around. "Couple of weeks. Knock out a few walls, check the basement and all the fixtures. Then we'll have a better idea of what needs to be replaced. Bad thing about pipes is you never know when they're going to spring a leak."

The most wicked thought skipped through her head and her cheeks burned as if he could read her mind. She cleared her throat. "I see."

"You have a special interest in the top floor? I generally start from the bottom and work my way up."

Was he playing with her head or was her underutilized sex drive acting up? "Actually, yes. I'll be moving onto the top floor once it's finished."

"I didn't realize that." He frowned for a moment. "I thought you said you lived nearby."

"I do…but I'll be selling my house."

"Then if that's what you want, that's what you'll have. It'll be pretty noisy around here while we're working. This whole project will take a couple of months at best."

"I'm sure I'll get used to it. You won't be working nights, I'm sure."

He grinned. "I've been known to work nights to get a job done."

Oh lawd. "That's good to know." Where could she run and hide before she said or did something really dumb? "Well—" she pulled her jacket tighter "—I'd better let you get to it." She turned to leave.

"Elizabeth?"

She turned. "Yes?"

"Are you seeing anyone?"

"What?"

"Are you seeing anyone?"

"Um, no." It was the truth.

"Good."

She stared at him for a moment, waiting for something else, but the something else never came. She went out the door and downstairs.

When she got outside she drew in a long breath. She glanced over her shoulder and Ron stood at the top of the steps in the doorway, fully and totally all man. "Ohmygoodness." She hurried off, jumped into her car and drove away, not having a clue as to where she was going.

Elizabeth drove around the neighborhood for a good hour, steering clear of the house, until she finally decided to give Barbara a call and see if she could take an early lunch.

"Girl, I wish I could get out of here early. My caseload is stacked today," Barbara said. "Why, what's up? Is everything okay with the house? Did the workmen show up?"

"Oh, they showed up, all right." She eased into a parking space and turned off the engine.

"What does that mean?"

Elizabeth's mind shifted to Ron, the way he walked, talked, the way he looked at her, the things he hinted at.

"Hello?"

"Oh…sorry."

"Did something happen?"

"Not exactly. Well, yes…" She began telling her about Ron and her out of body experience with him.

Barbara giggled on the other end. "Ellie, sounds like Mr. Man is interested."

"But I'm married."

"You're getting a divorce."

"I know, but…"

"But nothing! You need some excitement and happiness in your life."

"You really think so?"

"I know so."

"Maybe it was my imagination."

"What if it wasn't?"

"You're a grown woman. You know when a man has an interest in you."

"It's just been so long."

"All the more reason to see where it can go. It'll do you good."

Elizabeth smiled. "Listen to you. Is this the same woman who only months ago was in my shoes?"

"Hey, a little good loving goes a long way to changing a woman's mind about a few things."

Elizabeth giggled. "Did I mention that the man is fine? All caps?"

Barbara cracked up laughing. "Yeah, girl, you sure did."

Chapter 29

Ann Marie and Raquel walked out of the doctor's office in silence and headed to Ann Marie's car that was parked in the lot.

"I'm scared, Mama."

"Don't be. I'm sure everything will be fine. Dr. Harris said the results will be back in three days. No point in fretting about it now."

"I guess you're right."

"Have you spoken with Earl?"

Raquel shook her head. "Nothing to say."

"Just so 'ard to believe. I could skin 'im."

"Imagine how I feel."

Ann Marie glanced at her daughter. She was a beautiful girl. She'd been a beautiful baby, sweet from the day she was born, and never gave Ann Marie a spot of trouble. It was almost as if she sensed that she needed to be the best child possible to stay out of the way. Raquel had done everything right: got good grades, went to college, got a good job and married a handsome man. And now, none of that seemed to matter.

They got in the car.

"Thank you for coming with me. I don't know if I could have done it by myself."

Ann Marie nodded. "It's gon' be fine." She pulled out of the lot. "I have to go over to the house."

"The house?"

"Yes, the one—" She stopped when she realized she'd never told her daughter about her endeavor. "We purchased a house." She began to tell her about the night the idea was conceived and how far they'd come since then.

"That is so wonderful. Would you mind if I came with you…just to look? I promise I won't get in the way."

Ann Marie's heart seemed to twist in her chest with sadness. Here her daughter was twenty-three years old and still worrying that she might be in the way. Had she done that to Raquel? Had she been that lousy a mother?

"Sure. You can come."

Raquel beamed as if she'd been given a gift.

When they arrived at the house, the work crew were like bumblebees. They were all over the place. Debris was piled high in the front yard and an enormous dump truck was parked in front of the house. Ann Marie spotted Ron through the window on the top floor. She waved.

"Come on, let me show you around."

"Are you sure it's safe?" Raquel asked, stepping around big bins of trash and sweaty, dusty men.

"It should be fine." She led the way inside, pointing out the different rooms to Raquel as they made their way up to the top floor.

Ron spotted them standing in the doorway.

"Ann Marie." He smiled and came toward them. "I would shake your hand, but I'm kinda filthy." He chuckled. "Came to check up on us?"

"Of course. And I wanted to show my daughter around."

Ron looked at Raquel. "Your daughter? Nice to meet you." He swept his hard hat from his head and tucked it under his arm. "I'm Ron Powers, the foreman."

"Your guys are pretty busy," Raquel said.

"There's plenty to do around here, as you can see."

"Wow…all the original work," Raquel said in awe as she ran her hand along the mantel, checked the molding and the flooring. She didn't have words for the stained-glass windows, chandeliers and cathedral ceilings. "Mama," she said with reverence lacing her words, "do you truly realize what you have here?" She grabbed her mother's arm, something she hadn't done since childhood. "You see those moldings and the intricacy of the art in the stained glass?"

Ann Marie's expression was a cross between confusion and trying to keep up. "I...yes, I see them, but what about them?"

She turned her mother away from Ron. "There are only one hundred houses in existence that have that craftsmanship. The value is immeasurable. It's the work of Herbert Wilkes. He was one of the few black artisans that worked on these brownstones back in the early 1920s."

Ann Marie frowned. "How do you know all of this?"

Raquel looked at her askance. "I majored in fine arts, Mama. I have a bachelor's degree in fine arts and interior design. And a master's in art history. I sit on planning boards and committees that do restorations."

"What?"

Raquel grinned, put her hands on her hips and looked around. "Yep, I restore these beauties to their original splendor."

"Do you think you can do that with this house...and we'd still be able to run the spa?"

Raquel looked around again, slowly nodding. She walked out into the hallway and glanced up the stairs, walked down the hall and into the back room. She turned to face her mom, her expression resolute.

"If you give me the chance to work on this house, I guarantee you it will be exquisite...with nothing else like it." She began explaining what would need to be done, how she would need to work with the construction crew, materials to be used.

Ann Marie's heart filled. Who was this child/ woman who stood before her, confident and self-assured, talking about stains and finishings, mold-ings, restoration techniques and artifacts? It was her child, her Raquel, who she knew nothing about. She swallowed over the lump in her throat. It was time that she did.

"If you say you can do it, I believe you, chile. Let's talk it over with Barbara, Ellie and Steph later this evening."

Suddenly Raquel had her mother in an embrace, holding on for dear life. "Thank you, thank you, Mama. I'll do a good job, a great job. I promise you."

She buried her face in her mother's shoulder and for an instant Ann Marie wasn't clinging to her grown daughter but her tiny baby girl that needed her, depended on her. She promised herself that she wouldn't let Raquel down ever again.

They all decided to meet at Delectables for dinner and a battle plan.

"So it's really more of a treasure than we first thought?" Barbara asked Raquel, secretly tickled that Ann Marie had included her lovely daughter.

"Definitely," Raquel said.

"We're going to have to talk, Raquel," Stephanie said. "You'll be able to give me some buzzwords to punch up the promo for the opening of Pause."

"Not a problem."

"How can we help?" Dawne and Desiree asked in unison.

Elizabeth turned to her daughters then to her business partners. "We did say we would be serving healthy foods to our male guests?"

Everyone nodded.

"You can be our official caterers."

The twins clapped.

"We'll create specialties," Dawne said.

"Yes! And we'll come up with some really cool male names for the health shakes," Desiree said.

"I am so excited," Barbara squealed, clapping her hands together. "This is really going to happen."

"Yes!" Ann Marie seconded, looking into her daughter's shining eyes.

They all held hands.

"To health," Barbara said.

"To success," Stephanie added.

"To men!" Elizabeth shouted.

They all stared at her for a moment in shock before bursting out in joyous laughter.

"To men!" they all cheered.

Chapter 30

"So Ron and his crew are working out?" Michael asked Barbara.

"Yes, they're doing an incredible job. I can't believe how much they've done in just a few weeks. We can't thank you enough for the recommendation."

"Not a problem. I'm just glad it's working out."

Barbara stretched out on the bed, hugging the phone to her ear. Michael had been gone for nearly a month, the longest stretch of time they'd been apart.

"When will you get another break?" she asked.

"I wanted to surprise you, but since you asked… I'm downstairs."

She sprang up in bed. "Don't play with me."

He chuckled just as her doorbell rang. "Answer your door."

She darted past her mirror, stopped and doubled back. "Grrr." She hadn't had time to go to the hairdresser. She smoothed her hair back into a ponytail. The bell rang again. She tossed down the phone and ran to the door, thankful this time that the damn front door was still broken. She pulled the door open and her insides sang in delight. She leaped up into his arms and he spun her around like those heroes in musicals.

"Hey, baby," he crooned before claiming her lips for a long-overdue kiss.

Barbara sighed against his mouth, realizing how much she'd missed him, missed the feel and taste of him.

Reluctantly he set her on her feet. "Good to be back." His eyes roved over her like a hungry man ready to feast. "You look great."

"You need glasses." She giggled, took his hand and pulled him inside. "Why didn't you tell me you were coming?"

"I wouldn't have been able to surprise you, baby, if I'd told you."

"Very funny."

"How long will you be here?"

"A week."

She pouted. "That's it?"

"For now. The exhibition season starts in three weeks, so I have to get back."

She nodded then turned to him with a wicked look in her eyes. "Guess we're gonna have to squeeze in a bunch of fun stuff in a week."

"I just love how you think."

Barbara grinned. "Have you eaten? Can I get you anything?"

"No, thanks. I ate a little something before I got on the plane. But…I'd love a hot shower." He winked.

"Ohhh, really?" Slowly she rose, pulling him up with her. "Well, let me show you where the bathroom is. As a matter of fact, why don't I help you get out of all those clothes."

She started with his sweater that she pulled over his head and tossed on the chair as she backed her way toward the bathroom.

They left a trail of clothing en route to the bathroom. Michael turned on the shower until the room filled with steam.

Barbara and Michael played with each other in the steamy confines of the room. The hell with her hair, she thought as he nibbled on her ear and stroked her neck with his lips.

This time Barbara vowed to let go of the last of her inhibitions and be the aggressor. She wanted to see what that kind of power felt like. She eased Michael back toward the commode, flipped the cover down with her foot and made him sit down. A slow grin spread across his mouth.

"Oh, it's like that," he said.

"No, more like this." She took him slowly into her mouth and he actually gasped and grabbed her shoulders, sucking in air through his teeth. She slid her tongue along his length, memorizing the texture, the pulse.

"Welcome home," she whispered as she slowly rose to stand above him.

He gazed up at her through dreamy eyes. "If coming home is going to be like this…"

"The best is yet to come." She eased herself down onto him until he filled her. Resting her head against his shoulder, she sat perfectly still, embracing the feel of him. Then ever so slowly she began to move in rhythmic circles. His body shuddered as he pushed upward, but Barbara kept the pace slow and steady, letting it build.

Michael cupped the fullness of her breasts in his hands, flicking his thumbs across her nipples until she whimpered, then took one then the other into his mouth.

Barbara felt light as air as she finally relinquished control and let him move at will, bouncing her up and down on his shaft.

Somehow he managed to slide his hand between her legs and massaged her clit as she continued to ride him. Lights exploded behind her lids as one delicious sensation after another shot through her.

A strangled cry rushed from her throat as she climaxed so hard she was sure she'd blacked out for a moment.

Michael caressed the curve of her spine then

clamped her behind in his large hands, holding her firmly in place as he pushed and erupted inside her.

They clung to each other, the only sounds the rushing water and the rapid banging of their hearts.

Finally, when she was certain she had enough strength in her legs to stand without falling, she slowly stood up.

"Guess we'll be needing that shower now," she said, breathless and satiated.

They made a game of drying each other off then wrapped themselves in towels and went into the kitchen.

"So what is your role going to be in this endeavor?" Michael asked as they worked together in the kitchen, fixing a light after-the-loving snack.

"Well, I'll be administering the massages and working with the clients on the various machines, taking blood pressures. Making sure they are in good shape. Doing some processing of applications. A lot of what I'm doing now."

Michael grew silent.

She gave him a curious look as she sprinkled some grated cheese on their salad. "Something wrong?"

"Naw," he said. He took up the salad bowl and walked over to the table.

Barbara shrugged, tossing the odd behavior aside. "And I also have to select the equipment." Her face brightened. "Since you're here, maybe you can go shopping with me tomorrow to pick some things out."

He put some salad in a bowl and poured much too much dressing on it. "Yeah, sure." He kept his gaze averted, intent on his salad.

Barbara put her fork down. "You want to tell me what's suddenly bugging you?"

"I said nothing!"

She jerked back from the force of his words. "Fine." They ate in silence.

"Look, I need to go. I haven't even checked into my hotel and I have some things to do. Coach wants to be sure he can get to us if necessary." He got up from the table and practically tossed his bowl in the sink. He stalked out back into the bedroom and got dressed without saying a word.

Barbara stood in the doorway watching him as he got dressed. "You're acting very childish. How can I know what's going on if you don't say anything."

He turned on her as if she'd cursed his mama. "What? Childish?" He sputtered a nasty laugh. "I was wondering how long it would take for that to come out."

"Mike, what in the hell is wrong with you?"

"Like I said, nothing is wrong. And if you think I'm childish then so be it. I'm out." He brushed past her and was out the door before she could blink three times.

She shook her head in disbelief. What had just

happened? One minute they were making love like wild rabbits, the next he has his jockstrap twisted in a knot.

Sighing, she began picking up her clothing from the various places off the floor, then put them in the hamper in the bathroom. She went into the kitchen and started cleaning up, going over the events of the evening, trying to pinpoint where things had taken a wrong turn. For the life of her she couldn't figure it out.

By the time she settled down for bed it was nearly 1:00 a.m. She was sure she would have heard from Michael by now, apologizing and explaining his erratic behavior. As she stared up at the darkened ceiling, listening to the minutes tick by, the phone never rang.

The first thing she did the following morning was check her phone to make sure it was working. It was and there were no messages she'd missed. She dug in her purse for her cell phone. Again, not a word from Michael. She didn't even know what hotel he was staying in, or for that matter, if he was still in New York. If he could suddenly shift gears like that there was no telling what he might do on the spur of the moment.

That whole notion disturbed her as she fixed a breakfast of wheat toast and scrambled egg whites. From the beginning it was Michael who pursued this relationship. It was Michael who insisted that it would work out between them. He was gung ho. With great reluctance and a great deal of prodding from her friends she'd given in. As wonderful as things were between them, in the back of her mind she still had some reservations about their age difference. By the time he was forty she would be in her sixties. Where she had been married, he never had. And she knew that at some point he would want to settle down and probably have a family.

She sighed as she spooned her food onto a plate. She had to be realistic. This relationship, as eye-opening and liberating as it was, had a limited life span. And if his odd behavior last night was any indication of what a future with him would be, maybe the life span would be shorter than they'd both anticipated. One thing she'd learned in her forty-nine years was that she'd developed a low tolerance for crap, and the older she got the less crap she was taking.

"Just out of the blue he got all funny acting?" Elizabeth asked as she and Barbara walked through the sporting equipment supply outlet.

"Yes." She snapped her fingers. "Just like that."

"Hmm. Well, one thing I learned and learned the hard way is that if you don't have communication you are in deep trouble."

"Speaking of trouble, how are things working out with you and Matt?"

Elizabeth sighed. "It's in the lawyers' hands now. The upside is, the house is in my name and my name only. We never had it changed. So, the house is currently on the market. And the way real estate is going these days, it could be sold in a matter of weeks."

"Wow."

"So I'm really hoping that the contractors will at least be finished with the electrical and plumbing soon so that they can get started on the top-floor apartment. I don't want to move in with the girls, and threesomes are not my thing," she added, giving Barbara a wink.

"Very funny. After we finish here we'll go over to the house and see how things are going and talk to Ron about some realistic guesstimates."

Elizabeth smiled.

"Give you a chance to see Mr. Front Cover again. As a matter of fact, as your best friend in the world, I'll let you do all the talking."

Elizabeth giggled like a teenager. "Any excuse works for me."

"Girl, I've never heard you talk like that," Barbara said, tickled for her friend.

Elizabeth turned to Barbara, resting her hip against a workbench. "You know, I think that for at least the past ten years I've been sleepwalking through life."

Barbara checked the price on a massage table.

"Everything was routine. No excitement, nothing out of the norm." Elizabeth shrugged. "I convinced myself that I was content." She drew in a breath. "Maybe I can't blame Matt. He was probably feeling the same way. Somewhere along the line we forgot to be the people who fell in love with each other. We stopped talking, stopped doing anything that wasn't connected to the house or the girls."

"But you always seemed so happy."

"Looks can be deceiving. I had all the trappings of a successful marriage. And I convinced myself that it was a success. But day by day it was eroding and I was too blind to see it or maybe I didn't want to." She shrugged again. "That's why I'm saying to you, if you have communication problems now, nip them in the bud, they can only get worse."

Barbara thought about it as she placed an order for three massage tables, storage cabinets and blood pressure cuffs, and knew that her friend was right.

Chapter 31

Now that she was officially unemployed, she couldn't very well sit around all day in her pajamas, Stephanie thought as she exited her bedroom for the first time that day.

She padded into the kitchen to scrounge around for something to nibble on. She'd made an appointment to meet with Raquel and the twins at two to work out the promotional campaign and it was already noon. She had some ideas, but with Ellie's girls and Ann Marie's daughter now on the team she wanted their input.

Interesting, the dynamics between Ann Marie and her daughter, Stephanie thought as she popped two pieces of bread into the toaster. Something was going on between them, for sure. Ann Marie had barely mentioned her daughter in the years that they'd all known each other, but now Ann Marie and Raquel seemed to have made some kind of connection. Maybe that even accounted for Ann Marie's sudden change from bitch to human being. Whatever it was, she hoped it lasted. Ann Marie could certainly use some humanity in her life.

She buttered her toast and sat down at the kitchen table just as the phone rang. She pushed up from the table to get the phone and couldn't have been more stunned if she'd been smacked by a complete stranger.

"Annie? What's up?"

"I just received the paperwork in the mail to incorporate Pause for Men, and…uh, I was thinking that since you aren't…working, well, you, uh, mentioned something about doing your own thing…."

Ann Marie was a lot of things, Stephanie thought as she listened and wondered where the conversation was going, but hesitant about what she had on her mind wasn't one of them.

"Yes?"

"Well, I thought that maybe, if you were interested, of course, I could help you get your paperwork in order."

Stephanie pinched her thigh good and hard until she wanted to yelp. Nope, this wasn't a dream. "Say what? You want to help me?" She tossed her newly done weave over her shoulder to make sure not a word was muffled.

"Hey, maybe it wasn't a good idea, just a thought. Forget it, mon."

"No, wait. I'm sorry. It's just that…let's be honest for a minute, Ann…you and I have been like oil and water for years. You get on my last nerve and I get on yours. So, to say that this offer of yours is a surprise would be an understatement, that's all." She paused, swallowed her pride and decades of bad feelings. "So...what were you thinking?"

As she listened to Ann Marie her excitement grew. The idea of running her own business had been an idea she'd been toying with even before her abrupt resignation. But to hear someone, especially Ann Marie who had so much business savvy, say that she believed in the idea meant more to her than she could have ever expected.

"...and to cut down on overhead, at least until you get too big, and I can't stand you again, I thought it would be ideal if you worked right out of the house. Remember the room..."

Stephanie's mind was running at light speed. She could see it all as plain as her hazel contacts. The location was perfect, she'd have the chance to meet all manner of potential clients and wouldn't have to worry about rents or leases, at least for a while.

"I love it," Stephanie said. "I'm convinced."

Ann Marie laughed. "I could sell you your own damn panties and make ya t'ink they was new. I'm good, girl."

Stephanie heard a lightness in Ann Marie's voice, a playfulness that was foreign to her ears. And for once she wasn't offended by Ann's off-color comment.

"So what do I need to do?"

"Pick a name for one t'ing. I'll do a search and make sure it's not taken, and then we fill out the forms for incorporation."

"Ann?"

"Yeah…"

"Thanks. I mean that. I'm not sure if you fell on your head recently, if it's holy intervention or if Phil's been hitting all the right spots lately, but…"

"There's no more Phil."

"What? Why? I thought he was the one."

"So did I."

"Well…if you, uh, ever want to talk about it…"

"I'll keep that in mind." She pushed out a sigh. "Gotta get back to work. Me chat wit' ya lata."

"Sure. Thanks." She slowly hung up the phone, still in shock over Ann Marie's one-eighty. But it was all good.

No more Phil. Wonder what happened with that, and Ann never did say why Raquel and Earl split up. She shrugged it off. Everyone had their issues and she had enough to sink an ocean liner. But no time to dwell on things she couldn't change at the moment. She had to focus on what she could handle, the rest would have to wait.

Stephanie got dressed, packed up her trusty laptop and headed out, only to run smack into Conrad, who was standing outside her door.

"What are you doing here?"

"I want to talk to you."

"We have nothing to talk about."

She tried to walk past him but he grabbed her upper arm.

"Steph, please, hear me out."

She glared down at his hand on her arm. He removed it and took a step back.

"You have two minutes starting right now."

"I want you back."

"You have lost your mind."

"Maybe I have and that's why I was acting like such a fool. I'm sorry—for everything."

"Great. Now I have to go."

"I didn't mean the things I said in the office."

She looked him square in the eye. "Of course you did, Conrad. You never say things you don't mean."

"I did that day. I swear it. I was angry and quite frankly surprised."

"Surprised that I finally stood up for myself and stood up to you?"

He hesitated. "No. Surprised that you would leave. You're good at what you do. If nothing else, the firm needs you."

"I'm sure you'll find someone else to fill my shoes in no time."

"That's not possible."

She was tired of the conversation. "Your two

minutes are up. I have to go." She walked toward her car.

"What are you going to do for money? Where are you going to go and get the kind of clientele you've been dealing with since you've been with me?" he called out to her back in a last-ditch effort.

She used the remote and deactivated the car alarm. She opened the door.

"I love you, Stephanie."

She nearly stumbled.

"There, I've said it. I love you. I've made some awful mistakes. But I don't want to lose you. I'll make it all up to you I swear."

Their time together flashed through her head. The fun, laughter, the great sex, the hurt, the humiliation, the assault. She spun toward him. "I don't love you, Conrad. Maybe I did once. But I don't now and never will again." She opened the car door and got in, shutting it solidly behind her.

She watched him through her side-view mirror, standing there looking broken, the puff in his chest deflated. She had an instant moment of angst, a flash of possibility. The light turned green. Her new future lay ahead of her, the past behind.

She drove off and didn't look back. But in a corner of her mind she knew she hadn't heard the last of Conrad.

Chapter 32

When Barbara and Elizabeth arrived at the brownstone, the crew was just breaking for lunch. The men were in various states of relaxation as they walked inside.

"Excuse me," Barbara said to one of the men sitting on a huge can of plaster, eating a sandwich. "Is the foreman around?"

He lifted his hard hat back up on his head to better see them. He resembled a buffed Don Johnson, the actor, right down to the sparkling blue eyes and devilish grin. "He's working on the top floor. Said something about it being a rush."

"Thanks," Barbara said, and took Elizabeth's arm. "Girl, are they all this fine?"

"Honey, we don't need to open the spa for men, we could just let these guys keep working here forever."

They giggled and headed up the stairs. There were at least twenty men on the crew, ranging in age from early twenties to late forties, all fine, fit and delicious.

There should be some kind of law against having this many gorgeous men of every nationality in one location. They had to force themselves not to stare as the men bent, lifted, heaved and hoed.

"Lawdhavemercy," Barbara murmured.

"Must be like firemen," Elizabeth whispered as they reached the top floor. "You ever notice how every fireman is fine? Makes you almost want to set your house on fire just so they could run through there."

Barbara burst out laughing. "Ellie, you need to stop. I never knew you had your eye on other men."

"I may be married but I'm not dead or blind."

"I hear that." She lowered her voice. "There's your Mr. Fixit." She angled her chin in Ron's direction. He was up on a ladder, refinishing the molding in the front room. "I'll just make myself scarce. Go do your thing."

Elizabeth tugged in a breath at Barbara's encouraging smile. She walked toward Ron.

"Hey," she said, stepping up alongside the ladder.

He looked down and a smile of pure delight lit up his face. "Hey, yourself. This is a surprise." He came down, jumping off the last two steps. "How are you?" He wiped his hands on his dusty jeans.

"I'm good." She looked around, amazed at how much had been accomplished. "The place looks great."

He nodded. "We should be finished up here by the end of the week. We put in a new bathroom, rewired, stripped the floors and all the woodwork and replastered the walls. All that's left to do now is stain all the wood, shellac the floors and paint. As soon as everything is dry you can move in." He wiped the sweat from his brow with the back of his hand. "Have any particular color you want in the rooms?"

"I haven't really thought about it, but I guess I should at the rate you're going."

"Wanna take a walk-through, see what we've done? Then maybe the color scheme will come to you."

"Sure."

Barbara watched them walk off and she couldn't remember the last time she'd seen her friend look so lighthearted and happy. There was actually a sparkle in her eyes. How could they have been so close for so long and she not notice that Elizabeth was not really happy?

She supposed the same could be said of her. You simply get comfortable in a lifestyle and accept it. Like Ellie said, you convince yourself that you're happy simply because the bills are paid and the lights are on. But there is so much more to happiness than material things. Happiness starts from inside and works its way out. It's like a light that gets turned on in the dark, and like Ellie, the light shines in your eyes.

She'd known happiness with Marvin. She'd found happiness again with Mike, although a different kind. With Marvin, it was a satisfying kind of love. The kind of love you have for the man who makes you feel secure and protected. He was her second and only lover until Michael.

Where Marvin was conservative and very conventional, Michael was just the opposite. It would have never occurred to Marvin to perform oral sex, or make love in the shower or on the living-room floor. And she'd accepted that. She'd certainly never discussed her sex life with her girlfriends, even though they didn't seem to have a problem sharing theirs, especially Ann Marie.

Whether she and Michael worked things out or not, there was one thing she would always be grateful to him for: bringing her out of the dark and opening her up to her own sexuality and accepting it, embracing it without being ashamed of her desires or fantasies.

She smiled to herself. She liked sex—a lot. And she intended to have more of it. If she could catch the eye of someone as young as Michael Townsend, then the sky was the limit.

"What are you grinning about?"

Barbara blinked back into the present to see Elizabeth and Ron standing in front of her. Her face grew hot, as if they could read her thoughts.

"Oh, uh, just real pleased with how things are going."

"Good. We're working as fast as we can," Ron said.

"When do you think you'll be done?"

"Well, like I was saying to Ellie, we'll be finished

up here by the end of the week. The rest of the house will take about a month and we should be done."

"A month! Wow. That means we should be ready to open by July."

"The biggest job will be shoring up the foundation to accommodate the steam room and Jacuzzi. But I don't see it as being a problem." He checked his watch. "I better get back to work. I don't want the guys to think the boss is loafing." He grinned then turned to Elizabeth. "So, Sunday afternoon?"

Elizabeth nodded. "About two."

"I'll meet you out front." He stuck out his hand to Barbara. "Good to see you again."

She shook his hand. "You, too."

Ron walked away and started giving directions to the two men on his team.

"Sunday?" Barbara quizzed in a pseudo whisper.

Elizabeth giggled. "Yes, we're going to have brunch."

They headed back downstairs and out.

"Brunch is definitely a safe bet. Dinner lends itself to other things."

"Yes, and I want to take it slow. I don't want to rush into anything."

"He seems really nice and the way he looks at you…"

Elizabeth blushed. "It sure feels good, girl."

"I know what you mean."

When Barbara returned home, the first thing she did was check her messages. Still not a word from Michael. Her head was hurting a bit so she took two of the prescribed pills that the doctor had given her and decided to take a little nap.

When she awoke she was surprised to see that it was dark. She glanced at the bedside clock. She'd been asleep for nearly five hours. Stretching, she pulled herself out of bed, still fully clothed. That was the one drawback from those pain pills—they packed a real punch.

She went into the living room and turned on the television. Yawning loudly, she flipped through the channels, finally settling on the news. Her blood ran cold as she turned up the volume.

The newscaster was talking about a young woman who looked to be no more than twenty-five who had just left court in California to file a paternity suit against NBA forward Michael Townsend, the father or her two-year-old son Michael Jr. She claimed that he'd fathered the child when he lived in California and hadn't paid her child support in nearly a year.

Barbara felt ill. The camera zoomed in on the woman's face. She was stunning, long chestnut-brown hair, wide, expressive eyes and a body that she must work on 24/7.

Barbara instinctively pulled her sweatshirt down over her stomach and sat up a bit straighter.

They'd been college sweethearts, the report went on to say, and had lived together for several years. Mr. Townsend could not be reached for comment.

Barbara's stomach roiled. She flipped the channel and at the top of every broadcast was the story of NBA star Michael Townsend and the paternity suit.

Suddenly she jumped up from the couch, ran into the bathroom and threw up.

Finally pulling herself together, she returned to the living room and turned off the television. What a fool she'd been. She been so blinded by the fact that a young man would have an interest in her, she'd thrown caution to the wind and Michael had made a fool of her. She'd never asked him the questions she should have asked, like: Do you have any baby mama drama that I need to know about.

She pulled in a deep breath to calm the fluttering in her stomach. Well, good riddance, she thought. He can be someone else's problem as far as she was concerned.

Aimlessly she puttered around her apartment in a futile attempt to keep her mind off of Michael, to no avail. She was hurt, plain and simple. She'd been deceived and she didn't deserve that. She deserved an explanation and she was going to get one.

She went into the bedroom and dialed his cell phone. Her intention was to leave a nasty no-

nonsense message, but was almost at a loss for words when he actually answered.

"Before you say a word, Barbara, the baby is not mine."

"He has your name," she tossed out.

"And that's proof? Do you think I'm the kind of man that would shirk my responsibilities? I thought you knew me better than that."

"That's funny. I was thinking that I didn't know you at all."

"Please don't say that." He tone was plaintive. "Lacy and I have been down this road before. And now that I'm back playing ball she wants to cash in. It's as simple as that."

"There's nothing simple about it, Michael. She's filed a suit against you…in court."

"And the DNA tests will prove that I'm not his father."

"But she claims you stopped paying child support for the last year. The child is two. What about the first year?"

He breathed heavily into the phone. "When she told me she was pregnant I was suspicious then, but I went along with it. When she had the baby, I'd re-located to Miami when I got traded. I sent money. But when I went to see them about a year ago, she was with another guy, some bum she'd been seeing all along…even while we were together."

"So what?" She was becoming more pissed off. He wasn't making sense.

"The baby looks just like him. The two of them are in it together. Understand? Why should he take a dime out of his pocket when they can get it from me?"

Barbara took in the information. "So you're saying that the little boy is his and they're trying to get money from you?"

"Yes. That's what I'm saying."

"What if he isn't, Michael? What then?"

He was silent a moment. "If he is, which he isn't, I'll do the right thing by him, even if that means taking him from Lacy and raising him myself."

"How would you even manage something like that? You said yourself that you are on the road six to eight months out of the year. You're going to drag a little baby all over the country?"

"Not if I had a wife."

She actually heard her brain screech to a halt. "A wife?"

"Yes, a wife. You, Barbara. With or without the baby I want to marry you."

Whose life had she mistakenly stepped into? What the hell was he talking about? Marriage? To her? What?

"Michael…"

"Don't say anything now. Think about it. I'm leaving in the morning. My coach is going to arrange for the DNA test. We'll talk. I love you, no matter what you may think of me…and my childish ways," he added without rancor. "Think about it. I'll call you in a few days."

Barbara held the phone in her hand so long the dial tone buzzed in her ear.

Dreamlike, she hung up the phone. She looked around the room to make sure it was hers. Yes, everything looked familiar, but at the moment nothing else about her life resembled anything she could put her finger on.

Chapter 33

When Stephanie returned from her meeting with Desiree, Dawne and Raquel, she was feeling really good, her brief encounter with Conrad all but forgotten. The twins had some innovative ideas about the menu and how it would serve as a major appeal to the spa. And Raquel came up with some design ideas that would definitely set the tone and ambience that they were looking for.

She'd taken pages of notes and planned to spend the evening outlining the press release and begin designing the promo kit that she wanted to have available for the media and potential clientele. One of her approaches would be to connect with major corporations, most of which were headed by men. She was eager to get started. This would be her first major project that was not under the umbrella of H. L. Ruben.

She flicked on the lights in her apartment, changed into jeans and a T-shirt then settled down to work while the ideas were fresh and vibrant in her head.

They would definitely need a Web site, she thought as she began transcribing her notes. She knew some great Web designers and would make some calls within the next few weeks. Another thing she would need for the kits and the Web site were professional photographs of the house. Unfortunately those would have to wait until the construction was completed, and she definitely wanted them to include the shots of the decor that Raquel envisioned.

She'd been at it for a couple of hours when the phone intruded on her concentration. She muttered a curse under her breath, wishing that she'd remembered to turn the ringer off.

Reluctantly she got up from the desk and answered. "Hello?"

"May I speak with Stephanie Moore?"

Oh, damn, a telemarketer. "Who's calling?"

"This is Marilyn Hendricks, Conrad's wife."

The room spun for a second. "Who?" she sputtered.

"Conrad's wife. I take it you're Stephanie, the woman who's been screwing my husband."

"Look, you have the wrong number."

"I don't think so. I got it from Conrad."

"What?"

"He gave it to me. He claims that he's been trying to end the relationship and you won't leave him alone."

"I won't leave *him* alone! Are you crazy? Who is this?"

"I'm going to fight for my husband and my family no matter what it takes or how long. And you will get what you deserve for trying to destroy my family."

Click.

What the hell… More angry than bewildered, she hung up the phone. Conrad was stark raving mad and now she had to deal with his nutty wife. No telling what he'd told her and why. That was the real question: Why?

She turned and looked back at the phone as if it might reveal the answer to her question. She shook her head then went back to work. There were much more important things to worry about besides Conrad and…Marilyn. Gee, what next?

"How did the meeting go?" Ann Marie asked when Raquel came in.

Raquel hung up her jacket and walked into the living room where her mother was sitting, reading a book.

"Everything went really well. Stephanie is such a dynamic woman. She has some great ideas." She came and sat opposite her mother on the love seat.

Ann Marie marked her page and put the book down. "I've been doing some thinking."

Raquel sat up a bit straighter. "Yes."

"I know you don't think much of me as a mother…and neither do I." She smiled sadly. "Since you came back, I've been beating me brain trying to understand why it's been so 'ard to…"

"Love me?"

Ann Marie swallowed and looked away. "When I was a little girl growing up in Jamaica, we didn't 'ave much, ya know. Me mom she work for three families cooking, cleaning and watching other people's young ones. Not much time for me."

"Mom, you don't have to explain."

Ann Marie looked at her daughter. "Yeah, I do. I need to say some t'ings out loud. Most of the time I was left alone. Had to take care of myself for as long as I remember. It was a way of life, ya know. Mama would come home late at night too tired to be bothered wit' me. I learned to cook me own meals, wash clothes. Mama said only way me gon' know how to make it in the world is to do it on me own, stand on me own two feet. When I got some size on me and started lookin' more like a woman…" Her voice cracked. "Mama said since me be lookin' like a woman, I need to start ac'in' like one. She bring a man 'ome from the town said I be his woman from then on. She say can't be two women in she house." She sniffed hard. "I was only sixteen…a woman." She laughed a sad, bitter laugh. "Lost three babies wit' 'im 'fore you come."

Raquel's soulful brown eyes widened. Her mouth opened but no words would come.

"Your pop…he was older than me, a beautiful man. But he didn't know how to love no one but 'imself. Beautiful womanizer, Terrance Bishop." She looked at her daughter. "He spit ya out for sure."

Raquel bit down on her bottom lip to keep it from trembling.

"Took everyt'ing from me—me youth, virginity, hope and whatever love left in my heart. You come, I had not'ing to give, not'ing but the hard lessons I learned." She pressed her fist to her chest. "But he couldn't take me freedom. So I ran and been running since, running from anyt'ing gon' tie me down…including you."

Slowly, Raquel rose. "Thank you for telling me." Her eyes filled with water. She straightened her shoulders. "I'll leave. I'll find a hotel until I can get a place." She turned, stumbled then bent over and sobbed.

Ann Marie was behind her. She hesitated, her arms seemed unable to move. She willed them. And then her arms wrapped around her daughter, held her tight of their own accord. She absorbed the sobs, the pain, the years of loneliness and detachment. The dam finally broke and tears of release flowed from Ann Marie's eyes. Like the waters of baptism they cleansed her, renewed her spirit, healed her tattered heart.

Raquel turned into her embrace and held on. "We'll be all right now, Mama."

"I know. I know," Ann Marie whispered, and she believed it.

After a long silence, Rachel finally spoke. "I never really understood why you were so distant," Raquel said, sitting next to Ann Marie on the couch. She flexed her toes as she sat cross-legged.

Ann Marie poured a glass of wine and offered one to her daughter.

"Now I do, at least a little bit." She took the wineglass and sipped. "Can you tell me something about my dad? You've never spoken about him."

Ann Marie drew in a breath then exhaled slowly. "He was an officer on the island, well respected and a real charmer." She smiled at the memory. "He could charm you right out of your brand-new shoes. And so handsome when he smiled it would take your breath away."

"Why couldn't he make you happy?"

Ann Marie was thoughtful for a moment. "Terrance was much too absorbed to think about anyone else's happiness. It wasn't that he was unkind, he was…not there, only in body." Flashes of their unbridled lovemaking ran through her head. Terrance taught her everything she knew about sex. He taught her how to understand her body and give unimaginable pleasure to a man. But he never gave of himself, the one thing she desperately needed. So she took his lessons and mastered them. And when the time was right and Raquel was old enough to travel, she sought her freedom.

At first she was a doting mother. All Raquel had to do was squeak and Ann Marie was at her side. But as time passed and Raquel grew up, turned from plump innocent baby to enchanting pubescent girl, to a stunning woman, the spitting image of her father, Ann Marie's devotion waned with every passing year. By the time Raquel was ten, Ann Marie only did what was required: food, shelter, education. The more Raquel tried to cling, the more Ann Marie pushed her away until they were no more than two bodies sharing the same house and nothing more.

Raquel learned to iron her own clothes, cook, clean and check her own homework. She let herself in after school, prepared dinner and was sure to be out of the way by the time her mother got home from work. For the most part they rarely saw each other. On her eighteenth birthday she moved into her own apartment and married Earl right out of college. Ann Marie breathed a sigh of relief.

She wasn't quite certain when things began to change: her friends telling her not to choose a man over her child, seeing Raquel the morning she was crying in the kitchen, when she told her how Earl had betrayed her, or when Raquel grabbed her hand while they sat in the clinic waiting for Raquel's name to be called or when she discovered how talented Raquel was or maybe it was all those things rolled into one, a giant boulder that was finally able to break through the years of barricades she'd erected around her heart.

But things had changed, as much as she'd tried to fight it, tried to pretend that Raquel's plight was more of an annoyance than something she should deal with.

"Come." Ann Marie took Raquel's hand. "Let me show you a picture of your dad."

"You...you have a picture of him?"

Ann Marie nodded. She took Raquel into her bedroom and took down a box from the top shelf of the closet. She pulled out a tattered wallet and handed it to Raquel.

With shaky hands Raquel took the wallet and opened it. Her expression froze as she gazed upon the face so much like hers it was as if she looked in a mirror.

She ran her finger across Terrance's face. "Do you know where he is?"

"Hmm, Terrance was a wanderer. He could be anywhere."

"When was the last time you talked to him?"

Ann Marie swallowed. "Six months after you were born."

"He doesn't know where you are, where I am?"

"No."

"I don't know how I feel about that." She stroked the picture again. "I always believed that he just didn't care. But...if he didn't know where I was..."

She turned to her mother, her eyes filled with hope. "Maybe if I can find him—"

Ann Marie sprung up from the side of the bed. "No."

"What do you mean, no? Why not?"

"It was a lot of years ago, Raquel. Let it go. You know who he is. You've seen his picture. That's enough."

"Can I keep this?"

"Sure." Ann Marie pulled herself together. "I'm hungry. Let's fix something to eat." She left the room, feeling Raquel's steady gaze burn into her back.

Chapter 34

Barbara spent a sleepless night tossing and turning as images of newscasters ran behind her for her input on the Michael Townsend scandal that had her legs exhausted when she pulled herself out of bed.

What if it was a scam on the mother's part? It wouldn't be the first time, she told herself. She'd lost count of the numerous allegations made against athletes for one thing or another, only to find them baseless.

She brushed her teeth and stared at her reflection. He'd asked her to marry him. She spit out the toothpaste and rinsed her mouth. Married? She should be excited, a little bit thrilled, something. What she was without a doubt was confused.

Marriage was a big commitment. Not one to step into lightly. And she had to admit, if she was honest with herself, his timing was suspect at best. Did he ask because he really loved her or to distract her from what was really going on?

They hadn't known each other for even a year, at

least not as a couple. And to be honest, she wasn't crystal clear how she felt about Michael. Sure, she had the hots for him, she enjoyed his company, he made her feel good about herself, and he could definitely provide for her in a style to which she could easily grow accustomed. But did she love him?

She ran her fingers through her hair, noticing some new gray. In a matter of months, she would be fifty. Definitely in middle-age zone. She'd already begun to experience symptoms of menopause. It was only a matter of time before the clock struck midnight and she turned into a pumpkin. What then? How would he feel about her then, with vaginal dryness, crazy mood swings, hot flashes in zero-degree weather and her wanting to wear flannel pj's instead of Victoria's Secret to bed at night?

Yick, what a dismal picture. And what of children? It was too late for her, and if this child wasn't his, she was positive he would want a family of his own, something she could not provide.

She pulled her nightgown over her head and turned to face the full-length mirror that hung on the back of the bathroom door. She tugged in her stomach, stuck out her breasts and held her breath. Yeah, if she could walk around like this 24/7 she'd be a knockout. She exhaled before she got dizzy, and everything dropped unceremoniously back in place.

Face it, Barbara, she counseled herself, turning

sideways. You have the body of a mature, forty-nine-year-old woman, with big breasts, thick hips and a butt to gut ratio that was running a close race. The Barbie-doll woman at the gym assured her that she could tighten up her figure: with hard work, diet and exercise on Barbara's part. Truth was, she liked to cook and loved to eat. She hated treadmills, jogging, aerobics and perky gym instructors equally.

She glanced down between her legs and noticed a few straggling gray hairs down there, too. No, Ms. Clairol was not going "down there," that's for sure.

Sighing, she pushed open the shower stall and turned on the faucets.

Michael, Michael, Michael. What was she going to do? She stepped into the shower and momentarily the cleansing water washed away her troubling thoughts. At least for a bit.

While she was getting dressed her phone rang.

"Hello?"

"Barb, it's me, Ellie. Girl, I saw the news. I'm so sorry."

"Yeah, you and me both."

"Have you spoken to him?"

"I called him." She sat down in the wing chair in her bedroom. "He asked me to marry him…" She went on to tell Elizabeth about their conversation.

"I…I don't have a clue what to tell you. How do you feel about it?"

"I really don't know."

"Well, that can't be good."

Her other line rang. "Hang on a second." She switched over to hear Ann Marie blathering about "whuppin' 'is arse."

"Annie, listen, I appreciate the sentiment. But that won't solve anything."

"That's what ya all say. But a good arse whuppin' is just what some of dem need. I have a meeting, but I will call ya lata."

"Thanks, Annie." She switched back to Elizabeth. "It was Ann Marie. She suggests doing a drive-by."

Elizabeth giggled. "She would. Anyway, girl, I know you will do what's in your heart to do. Whatever decision you make, you know I'll support you."

"I know. Thanks."

"Look at the bright side, when was the last time a fine, thirty-something man asked you to marry him?"

"It's been a minute," she said, and laughed. "Hey, isn't today brunch with Ron?"

"Yes, it is."

Barbara could hear the smile in her friend's voice. "Well, you enjoy yourself and don't do anything crazy."

"That's what I have to keep telling myself…not to do anything crazy. Every time I see that man, my juices go into overdrive."

Barbara's eyes widened. Was this Elizabeth Lewis

talking? "Well, you just try to keep those juices under control, okay?" She smiled.

"We're going to a public place. He's meeting me at the restaurant. We're arriving in separate cars." She blew out a breath. "Can't get any more 'dry' than that." She giggled. "I swear, I don't know what's gotten into me lately."

Me neither, Barbara wanted to say but didn't. "My advice, go with the flow. You only live once, so enjoy it for as long as it lasts."

"Yes, I deserve some happiness." She paused. "And so do you, Barbara. Whether it is with Michael or a mystery man you have yet to meet. It's been a lot of years since Marvin, a lot of years not to have someone in your life. I know it can't always be easy."

"It hasn't been. I was lonely a lot of the time. Everyone seemed to have someone except me. But I kept myself busy and convinced myself that I was content."

"Like me," Elizabeth cut in.

"Exactly. So when I got involved with Michael, it was as if I became of full female for the first time in years. He made me appreciate my femininity, something that, as much as I loved Marvin, he never did."

"I'm sorry."

"Don't be. At least I understand it all now. And if nothing else, I have Michael to thank for that."

"Then it's a good thing."

Barbara smiled. "Yes, it is. Listen, you get ready for your date. Call me with all the details later."

"I will."

Barbara hung up, thoughtful for a moment. Hmm, darn right, a thirty-something, fine, rich man asked her to marry him.

She marched over to her closet and pulled out her workout clothes. So what if she hated perky gym instructors. If it wasn't Michael in her future, it might be the mystery man. But in any case, she would always have herself as her best friend and she wanted to be all that she could be—for her.

Besides, she could get some inside tips on running Pause for Men and what better place than a gym to scope out potential clients.

She giggled, grabbed her never-used gym bag and headed out.

Elizabeth felt like a teen going to her senior prom. Her palms were sweaty and suddenly her closet full of clothes all seemed inappropriate.

"Mom, are you ready yet?" Desiree called out from the living room. "It's getting late."

"Do you need some help?" Dawne shouted.

Elizabeth pulled open her bedroom door. "Yes! Help!"

Her daughters laughed and came running.

Desiree stood in the middle of the bedroom,

stunned by the pile of outfits that were dressing the bed instead of her mother. "I had no idea you had this many clothes. Wow."

"Gee, Mom, you could have a sale and make a mint," Dawne added in awe, picking up a Chanel sweater with pearl buttons. She held it up to herself and turned to the mirror.

"None of your commentaries are helping the situation," Elizabeth moaned. She snatched back her sweater. "Give me that."

"Touchy, touchy." Dawne squatted on the floor.

Desiree put her hands on her hips and made sweeping observations of the choices. "I say, go casual. You don't want him getting the wrong idea."

"Yeah, nothing too low or too short," Dawne chimed in.

"Forget the pantsuits." Desiree walked to the bed and plucked the half-dozen suits and put them to the side. "Nothing flashy." She took out the beaded designer sweaters and palazzo pants.

"Don't you have any jeans?" Dawne asked.

"Yes, but are jeans appropriate for a…date?" She barely got the word out.

"Of course!" the sisters said in unison.

"Jeans go with everything," Desiree said.

"As much as they cost these days, they better," Dawne added.

"So, let's go with black jeans, a nice boot with a

heel—you know the ones I love—the black suede, and you can dress it up with…" She scanned the bed and pulled out a baby-blue sweater set. She held it up. "This is perfect. Soft, feminine and in style."

Elizabeth's brow creased for a moment. "Are you sure?"

"Positive."

"Yeah, it says, I'm comfortable and sexy without being in your face with it," Desiree said, grinning.

Elizabeth blew out a breath, looking from one daughter to the other—perfect, gorgeous bookends. She was so happy and so lucky to have their support. When she told them she was going on a date, they didn't blink and they hadn't given her a moment's grief about the divorce. Matthew may be a jerk but he did give her two beautiful girls. For that she would always be grateful.

"Okay," Elizabeth finally conceded.

"Now, hurry up so you can go and get back and tell us what happened," Desiree said.

Elizabeth laughed. "I'll think about it." She started for the bathroom to change then stopped and turned. "I guess I should have told you before now, but I'm selling the house."

"You are? Why?" Dawne asked.

"It's a long story. I'll tell you both all about it when I get back."

"But, Ma, where are you going to live?"

She smiled. "At the spa. The top-floor apartment is ready and I'll be moving in by the end of the month." She spun away. "Ron's been working on it. It's perfect." She shut the bathroom door behind her.

Desiree and Dawne looked at each other in open-mouthed astonishment.

"Go, Mom!" they chuckled.

Her daughters' words of encouragement echoed in her mind as Elizabeth drove around the block several times before she was able to find a parking space. It was a beautiful early-summer afternoon, the kind of day that was warm enough to go without a jacket and still not bake in the sunshine. With summer under way, the residents of Manhattan and beyond were out in full force, pushing strollers, inline skating, bike riding, walking designer dogs, couples, singles and the mix-and-match. Everyone was taking advantage of the day, which meant that just about every seat at the outdoor cafés were taken.

She weaved in and out of meanderers in the direction of Isabelle's, a new restaurant on Ninety-sixth Street and Broadway. The girls recommended it, and if they gave it a thumbs-up, she was sure it was good.

As soon as she approached, she saw Ron standing outside waiting for her. He was looking in the opposite direction, which gave her a few brief moments to take him all in.

He, too, had chosen jeans, a lightweight leather jacket and a button-up oxford shirt in stark white underneath the jacket.

Yum, yum. Get a grip, girl. She drew in a breath and it all but stuck in her throat when he turned to her and the full wattage of his smile lit up the block. He walked toward her and, before she could exhale, he leaned down and kissed her lightly on the cheek.

His hand was at that low curve at the bottom of her back.

"You look great," he said.

"Thanks. So do you."

He chuckled. "Oh, this old thing."

Elizabeth laughed, breaking that knot that had wrapped itself around her stomach.

"Come on, I got us a table."

"Outside?"

"Absolutely. No point in coming to one of these places if you can't get an outside table. Nothing can compare to the sights you see going by during a meal."

He helped her into her seat. "I hear the food is great."

"That's what my daughters told me. And they would know."

He looked at her. "It's just so hard to imagine that you have two grown daughters."

"It's hard for me to imagine sometimes, too." She smiled.

"Let's order. Then we'll talk. I want to hear it all."

And she wanted to tell him, she really did. But the voice of wisdom, namely, her mother, whispered, *"Never tell a man everything, it takes the mystery out of being a woman."* For once she'd take her mother's advice.

She looked up as the waitress approached to take her order and saw Matthew coming in their direction.

Chapter 35

"Are you okay?" Ron asked, seeing the frozen expression on her face.

"Well, fancy seeing you here. You didn't waste any time, did you?"

Ron looked up at Matthew then across at Elizabeth. "Can I help you?"

"Seems like you already have…to my wife."

Ron pushed up from his seat, a slow scowl darkening his face. He cocked his head to the side. "Excuse me?"

"This is between me and Ellie."

"Only if she wants it to be."

Elizabeth reached across the table and grabbed Ron's wrist. "It's okay." She looked up at Matthew. "Why don't you continue in the direction you were heading, Matt. I'm trying to have lunch."

"Is that all you're having?"

Ron moved toward him. Elizabeth held tighter,

feeling the muscles in his arm tighten all the way
down to his fingertips.

"Matthew, leave."

He glared from one to the other. "Is this some
kind of payback?" He chuckled. "I would have
thought you could do better than this, Elizabeth."

This time Elizabeth couldn't hold on and the
next thing she knew, Ron had Matthew by his shirt
collar and had actually lifted him up off the
ground. If it weren't so utterly horrible, she would
have laughed at the petrified expression on Matthew's face.

The patrons at the two tables closest to them
jumped up from their seats and backed away.

Elizabeth was on her feet. "Ron, please, he's not
worth it." She grabbed his upper arm that felt like steel.

"If you ever say another word to this lady that isn't
pleasant, you'll have me to deal with. I promise you
that." He let him go and Matthew stumbled back-
ward, bumping into a passing couple.

Matthew coughed several times and tugged on his
shirt. He glanced around at all the peering eyes. His
chest was puffed up so big Elizabeth thought he
would explode.

"And to think I wanted you back." He threw her
one nasty look and stormed off.

Ron turned to her. "Are you okay?"

"F-fine," she stuttered, and slowly sat down.

"Can…we go someplace else?" She didn't dare look around at the scrutinizing eyes.

"Sure." He came around and took her arm. "Come on, let's go."

"I'm really sorry," she murmured as they walked down the street.

"Don't be. He's a jerk. It wasn't your fault."

"I never expected him to act like that."

"Why didn't you tell me you were still married?"

She swallowed. That little bit of wise advice about being mysterious was definitely biting her in the butt now. "I…I guess it's because I don't feel like I am. I know I should have said something to you. We're separated. He left me, months ago, for a younger woman." She laughed a sad laugh. "Our divorce will be final soon."

"How long?"

"Twenty-five years."

"Wow. I'm sorry. I know it has to be hard."

"I'm getting through it. I just want it to be over." She glanced up at him. "What exactly were you going to do to him, anyway?"

He grinned. "Toss him across the street."

Elizabeth giggled. "Did you see the look on his face."

"Yeah." He laughed. "It was kind of funny."

She blew out a breath. "Thanks for coming to my rescue."

"I don't tote all those barges and lift all those bales for nothing."

Elizabeth laughed and slipped her arm through his. "Know what? I'm starved. And I have the perfect place for us to eat."

"Lead the way."

"Girls, this is Ron Powers." Elizabeth turned to Ron and introduced her daughters.

"You two really are identical." He smiled and shook their hands.

"I'm Desiree. I'm really the cutest."

"I'm Dawne. Don't pay her any attention."

"I'll keep that in mind." He looked around. "Great place. Your mother told me about it, but it's much more than I expected."

"Thanks. We're really proud of it," Dawne said.

"She also says the food is great."

"Mothers never lie," Desiree said. "Come on, have a seat and we'll hook you right up." She showed them to a table.

Desiree brought over the menu. "We've added a few new things, Mom. We want to test them out on our customers before we introduce them at the spa, just to see how they go."

"Great."

"Well, take your time ordering. Let me or Dawne know when you're ready."

Ron studied the menu. "Nice girls. You must be proud." He looked at her.

"I am."

"How do they feel about the divorce?"

She set her menu down. "Let's put it this way, they helped me pick out my outfit."

He chuckled. "And they have good taste."

Elizabeth blushed.

Ron reached across the table and put his hand gently on hers. "Listen, whatever is going to happen between us, let's promise to be honest with each other. That way, no surprises, no disappointments. Deal?"

"Deal." She paused a moment. "So, is there something that you need to tell me?"

"As a matter of fact, there is…."

Elizabeth was sure she was running in the direction of her house, away from the restaurant, away from Ron, away from the I-don't-wanna-believe-it story he'd just told her. But, damnit, she hadn't moved. She couldn't. Her legs felt like lead and her heart was just as heavy.

"Jail?" Elizabeth expelled on a breath of disbelief. Her throat was so dry, that was all she could get out.

Ron clasped his hands on the table and slowly nodded his head. "I did eighteen months."

A felon! She would wind up with a felon. "When?" All sorts of ugly images ran through her head. She'd seen *Scared Straight* and several other prison movies, not to mention *Oz* on HBO. Prison! Oh Gawd.

"It wasn't yesterday, Ellie, not even the day before. It was when I was back in college."

She did a quick calculation in her head. That had to be well beyond twenty years ago, the seventies, late sixties…pre-AIDS. She was finally able to swallow and eeked out, "Oh."

"I was a member of the Black Panthers."

"What? You were?" She could see Ron with a black beret cocked to the side, with a machine gun hanging from his shoulder. Kind of gave her a little thrill. She remembered seeing photographs and news photos of the angry black men who wanted to "take it to America."

He nodded. "I was a student at the University of Mississippi. How black students were treated, how blacks in general were treated…" He shook his head at the memories. "Anyway, I was determined to do my part for the cause, to rally the young people together. I was holding meetings, sending out news-letters, printing flyers, recruiting." He blew out a breath. "Someone, and to this day I don't know who, went to the administration and the administration went straight to the FBI."

"Oh no."

"Anyway, one morning there was a knock on my room door, I was put in handcuffs and thrown in jail, charged with conspiracy."

"What?"

"That's how things went down back then. It took me nearly two years and a battery of charges to beat the case against me. But as a result, I wound up on the FBI's watch list."

"Watch list?"

"Yeah, every now and then I get a visit or a phone call, just to see 'how I'm doing'" He shrugged. "I'm used to it by now. Part of my life, but I wanted you to know, just in case we are together somewhere and a little man in a dark suit walks up to me."

"Sounds like something out of a spy movie." She wasn't sure if she was appalled or intrigued.

"And now with all the terrorist alerts, alarms, code oranges and the Patriot Act, I'm sure they're going to step up their game."

"What do you mean?"

"I've already been paid a visit at my apartment."

She leaned forward. "Do you think they would come to the spa?"

"It's possible. But I wouldn't worry about it. Once the job is finished, they would have no reason to come there. I'll be gone and they'll just follow me around like they've been doing for the past thirty-plus years."

"Wow, and I thought you were going to tell me something innocuous like you were allergic to shell-fish or something."

"Not shellfish, cats. You don't have cats, do you?"

Elizabeth laughed, snapping the rope of tension

that had wrapped around her throat as she'd listened to his story.

"No, I don't have cats." She looked at him. "Is there anything else I should know?"

"That's pretty much it. No secret babies, no ex-wife, no girlfriend. Pretty much what you see is who I am—a hardworking, honest man who wants things to be right in his life and in the world." He slapped his hand down lightly on the table. "That's my story."

"Thank you for telling me. I appreciate it."

"Is there anything else about you that I should know? Some gross habit?"

She chuckled lightly. "Unfortunately, my life is nowhere near as interesting as yours. I got married straight out of college, put my career on the back burner for my husband and my children."

"That can't be it. You make your life sound like you were a Stepford Wife. I can't believe that about you. What are your interests, hobbies, what career did you kick to the curb?"

"I wanted to run my own business. I wasn't sure what it was. I knew the things I loved, cooking and decorating. I know, it sounds so frivolous, but…"

"Not at all. What's wrong with doing what you love, what you enjoy? Look at me, I'm an over-grown kid getting to play with big trucks and hammers and drills."

"I guess you're right."

"So now that you have the opportunity to go after your dream, what are you going to do?"

Her expression softened, her eyes took on a sparkle. "I haven't spoken to the girls about it yet, but I was thinking that even though I'm the only one of the four of us who hasn't worked outside of the home, I'm the only with any real in-the-trenches managing skills, from scheduling to meals, to appointments, inventory. You name it. Running a household is like running a small company."

"So you want to be the spa manager?"

She nodded. "Yes."

"So, go for it. No one else has stepped up, have they?"

"No. We've all been so busy just getting the groundwork in place."

"Listen, when I decided I wanted to get into construction, I didn't have practical experience. I'd always been 'the other guy,' the 'go-to guy,' but never the head man in charge. I took out a loan, called on some guys that I'd worked with on some other jobs and went for it."

"What was your first job?" she asked, more intrigued by him.

"Don't laugh."

She made a sign of the cross. "Promise."

"My mom's basement."

"Everybody has to start somewhere."

There was a momentary pause when they looked into each other's eyes and then burst out laughing.

"And trust me," he sputtered, "your mama is your worst customer." He took a long swallow of his iced tea.

Elizabeth pulled herself together and wiped her eyes with the napkin. "I can only imagine."

"Well, I hope it's not our food you're both laughing at," Dawne said, stepping up to the table.

Ron looked up. "No, not at all. I was telling your mother about my first contracting job."

Dawne pulled up a chair and sat down, Desiree followed.

"Ron used to be a Black Panther," Elizabeth said with a sound akin to pride in her voice.

"Get out!" the girls chimed. "Tell us all about it. That is so cool."

It didn't take much prodding from the twins to get Ron to recount his youthful exploits as a 1960s militant. The young women were captivated.

"Looks like you've worked your charm on my daughters," Elizabeth said later, as they walked to their respective cars.

They stopped in front of Elizabeth's car. "You are the only one I'm looking to charm, but your daughters run a close second." He winked.

"I'll keep that in mind." She disengaged the alarm on her car and opened the door.

"So…have I scared you off?"

"Not yet," she said.

"Good. I want to see you again. You name the day and time."

"Fair enough." She got in the car, looked up at him. "Friday night. Eight o'clock."

The corner of his mouth lifted. "My treat, wherever you choose."

"We'll talk about it during the week."

"Planning on stopping by to check on me?"

"Actually, I'll be moving some of my things up into the apartment. I'm sure I'll need some help."

He leaned down, pressing his palms against the frame of the open window. "I did mention that I was a handyman?"

Elizabeth giggled. "See you during the week. Thanks for a great afternoon."

Ron stepped back, slid his hands into the front pockets of his jeans, forcing her eyes to that enticing bulge in his pants. She swallowed and dragged her eyes to his face. She put the car in gear before she said something really dumb like: Come-home-with-me-I-haven't-had-a-man-in-months. And as she watched him watching her through her rearview mirror, it took all her home training not to make a U-turn and a fool out of herself.

She couldn't wait to get home and call Barbara.

Chapter 36

Now Barbara was convinced beyond a shadow of a doubt that she hated perky little gym instructors more than any other creatures on earth.

She was sure she was dragging her left leg up the steps and that creak she kept hearing wasn't the stairs. If she thought for one minute that the very young and athletic Michael Townsend had whipped her body in directions she didn't know were allowed by law, he didn't have nothing on Ms. Girl at the Sports Spot.

Her muscles howled, calling her every name but a child of God. She didn't think she'd make it to the tub, and if she did, she'd probably sink beneath the hot water and drown. At least she would be put out of her misery.

Through pure force of will she made it into her apartment without collapsing. She tossed her hated gym bag into the corner, inched across the living room and plopped down on the couch.

The phone rang, beckoning her. She groaned, got

up and answered the phone. It better not be a tele-marketer, she thought as she said hello, 'cause they were sure going to get an old-fashioned cussing-out.

"It's Michael."

She sat down on the stool in the kitchen next to the phone. "Yes?"

"I was calling to see how you were doing."

"Fine," she lied, and tried to stretch out her leg without screaming.

"I was hoping that I could see you."

"See me? What are you talking about? You said you were in Miami."

"I am. But I'm leaving in the morning. We need to talk."

"I don't see where there is anything to say right now, Mike."

"Please, Barbara."

She sighed heavily, too tired to argue. "Fine. When?"

"I'll be getting in about noon tomorrow. Can I meet you at work for lunch? I have to get right back on a plane at six."

"I suppose so."

"Thanks. I'll see you tomorrow."

What could be so urgent? she wondered as she hung up the phone. He couldn't have gotten the DNA results back yet. Even the muscles of her brain were exhausted. Whatever it was, it would keep until tomorrow. For now she needed a hot bath with some Epsom salts.

Barbara's first patient the following day was Mrs. Wells. She was a treat and definitely the lift that she needed.

"How are you and that young man doing?" Veronica Wells asked as she ceremoniously disrobed. Veronica was notorious for doing a virtual strip show each time she came in for her appointment. If you got it flaunt it was her motto.

Barbara sighed, pulled the drapes and sat down on the stool that was in front of the exam table where Veronica was daintily perched as naked as she was born.

"Not so good at the moment," she confessed.

"Sorry to hear that. I knew something must be wrong, that spark is missing from your eyes." She heaved a sigh. "Do you think I should get a Brazilian wax? I hear it's all the rage."

There was no telling what Veronica would say at any given moment, but this was definitely up there in the top ten.

Barbara didn't dare answer. "Did you see the news the other night, the story about the basketball player and a pending paternity suit?"

Veronica frowned in thought. Then she brightened. "Yes, I believe so. Pretty little thing."

"Well, the man she wants to sue for paternity is the man I've been seeing."

"Oh." Veronica twisted her lips in consternation. She shrugged nonchalantly. "And what is the problem? Men screw around all the time. This one just happened to get caught. Doesn't make him a bad man, just careless." She angled her head to look at Barbara. "So...why are you really upset?"

Barbara huffed. "It's not so much that he had a life before me. I have a problem with him paying child support for a year and then stopping."

"Maybe he had good reason. Maybe he found out something that changed his mind."

Barbara chewed on her bottom lip. "I suppose."

"Did you talk to him about it?"

"Sort of. I was too upset to really make sense."

"Want my advice?"

Barbara nodded.

"See what happens before you make a decision. He may be totally vindicated. How many times are the claws put on athletes?"

"I know."

"What's important is how you feel about him, if the relationship is even important enough to pursue."

She looked into Veronica's eyes and told her about Michael's proposal, something she hadn't even shared with Ellie when she'd called to tell her about her harrowing date with Ron.

"Sounds like he's serious."

"Hmm."

"Well, dear, as I said, go with your heart. You have a good head on your shoulders, use that, too." She winked at Barbara and that made her smile.

"Thanks, Veronica."

"Anytime. Now, let's see how high I can get these legs up in the air. We're planning a seven-day Caribbean cruise and I want it to be a trip that my husband will never forget and I don't mean the food."

Barbara laughed and shook her head.

She was a nervous wreck as she stood in the hospital lobby waiting for Michael later that day. He'd called on his cell phone nearly a half hour earlier to say he was on his way. She checked her watch. Her lunch hour would be over in another fifteen minutes.

Although he was hard to miss at six foot six inches, she barely recognized him. He wore a baseball cap pulled low over his eyes, a hooded Nike sweat jacket and matching pants. She hated to admit it, but he really did look like one of the kids she saw running around in the park.

He pulled off his shades as he approached. "Sorry I'm late."

"Why are you dressed like that?" She was accustomed to him in casual attire, but he truly looked like a character from *Boyz in the Hood*.

"Where can we go to talk?"

"I really don't have much time, Mike. I have to get back to work. I guess we can go to the employee cafeteria."

"Fine." He took her arm. "Sorry it took me so long to get here. I wanted to make sure that no press were dogging me."

"Press!"

"Yeah, they've been all over me since the story broke. One of several reasons I needed to get out of Miami so I could breathe. I've been like a prisoner in my apartment."

It hadn't occurred to her how all this was affecting him and his life.

"I'm sorry. I didn't know."

"Not your fault." He looked down into her upturned face. "None of this is."

They continued down the corridor and turned right, toward the cafeteria. It was busy. No one paid them much attention.

"There's a table in the back," Barbara said, leading them to it.

Once they were seated, she launched right in. "What was so urgent that you needed to see me today?"

He dug around in his pocket, pulled out a box and put it on the table between them.

"Don't open it yet. Hear me out." He took a breath, collected his thoughts. "When you came into my life, not as my therapist but as a woman, my life changed, for the better. I know I may not be all that you want, but you are what I want. I've never been more sure of anything in my life. When I asked you to think about marrying me it was the biggest step I've ever taken in my life. I've never asked a woman to share my life. You are the first and I hope the last." He opened the box and Barbara's heart stopped short then beat at an alarming rate. "This is only a small token, something that I want you to hold on to while you think whether or not you want to share my life."

The diamond, sitting on a platinum band, was blinding in its brilliance. Light bounced off the stone in a kaleidoscope of colors. She didn't want to guess how many carats. This was Elizabeth Taylor action.

"Michael...I don't...can't..."

"Please, don't say anything. I don't want an answer. Take it. Think about it. And when the decision comes back from the test, whichever way it turns out, make your decision then. That's all I ask." He pushed the box toward her.

The diamond called out to her, *Take me, take me.* Trancelike, she reached for the box. She looked at him, looked at the diamond and closed the box.

"Michael, I can't take this from you."

"Why?"

"Because to me it's the equivalent of saying yes I'll marry you, and I haven't said that or know that I will."

He exhaled heavily and nodded his head in understanding. "Fine." He stood. "I need to get back to the airport, my flight was changed." He licked his lips. She handed him the box. He ignored it.

"I'll call you in a couple of days." He turned to leave.

"Michael!" She jumped up. Hc walked faster. She started off after him and noticed the eyes that were turning in her direction. The last thing she wanted was a scene and for the assemblage to actually recognize Michael, if they hadn't already. She slowed her step. In her moment of hesitation, Michael walked out and was gone.

Barbara straightened, gripping the velvet box in her hand. She slid the box into the pocket of her smock. A diamond bigger than her eye? What would the girls have to say about that?

She hurried back to her office, shut and locked the door behind her. Like a kid coming down too early on Christmas morning, she looked over her shoulder before opening the box. The diamond flashed in her eyes.

"My goodness," she said in awe.

Reverently she took it out of the box. This sucker was heavy, too. She tentatively slid it onto her ring finger and held her hand out in front of her. Perfect fit. She turned her hand slowly from side to side, watching the light dance off of it.

A slow smile crept across her mouth. "Damn, that looks good."

Chapter 37

Stephanie set up an interview with a photographer that would be taking pictures of Pause for the catalog and print material that she was putting together. He was actually one of the names she'd pulled from her Rolodex but had never used. Anthony Dixon. She'd checked out his Web site, which was impressive, but she was always one who believed in seeing things live. She knew the power of Photoshop. Someone skilled could make Medusa look like a runway model.

She sipped a glass of lemonade while she waited for him to arrive and flipped through her folder of things she still needed to do. They were scheduled to meet at two. She hoped he could convince her of his skills in an hour. She wanted to sit with her sister and have dinner with her if she was having a good day. And she had one more appointment before she could see Samantha.

"Ms. Moore?"

Stephanie looked up and hot damn it was Morris

Chestnut's dad or a darn good look-alike. He was a dead ringer for the actor or rather what the actor's father must look like: tall, chocolate dark and layered in the matured assurance of masculinity.

"Yes, I'm Stephanie." She stood and extended her hand.

"Anthony Dixon. Everyone calls me Tony," he said, taking her hand. He smiled. She stuttered.

"Glad…you could make it. My office isn't set up yet, so I hope this isn't an inconvenience."

"Not at all." He took a seat and put his portfolio on the table.

"You mention in your information that you do company brochures, logos, etcetera."

"Yes." He flipped open his portfolio and turned several sheets until he reached the sample he was looking for.

Stephanie was fixated on his lashes. They were inky black, long and gently curled. And there was a subtle, intangible, stirring scent that floated lightly around him. She felt compelled to move closer and inhale until her lungs were full. That is, until she spotted the simple gold band on that telltale finger.

Damn, damn, damn. What am I, some kind of married-man magnet? Is it written on my forehead?

"…this one is the corporate brochure I did for Virgin Records."

Stephanie snapped to attention. This was business.

Probably best that he was married. She would be forced to concentrate on the project and not what his lips would feel like brushing across her…

"What did you have in mind?"

"Excuse me, I'm sorry. What were you saying?"

He smiled and it nearly did her in. *Good teeth.*

"I was asking if you had any ideas in mind."

"Actually, yes. Let me give you some background on the project…."

They talked for more than an hour, her next appointment all but forgotten. Anthony was easygoing, intelligent, a brilliant graphic artist, as well as an accomplished photographer, and he gave her some good ideas. He'd worked for some of the major firms in the city, having started out as a copywriter at Ogilvy and Mather, one of the top ad agencies in the country. By the time their meeting concluded, she was sure she'd found the right person for the job.

Stephanie stuck out her hand. "If you're willing to take on four women, you have the job."

"I love a challenge." He shook her hand. "When can I get over to the house to take some preliminary shots?"

She turned on her Axim and used the stylus to check her calendar. "How's next Monday, about two?"

He turned on his Palm Pilot and confirmed. "Not a problem."

"Great." She checked her watch. "Oh no!"

"What?"

"I was supposed to meet someone nearly twenty minutes ago." She shoved her folder into her oversize shoulder bag and jumped up.

"Maybe you should give them, him, her a call." He handed her his cell phone.

"Right. Thanks." She took his phone even though she had one of her own. She punched in the number from memory and listened to it ring. His phone had his scent, too, she noticed as it floated to her brain.

"Hi, Sylvia. This is Stephanie Moore, I am so sorry…"

She breathed a sign of relief when she hung up. "We've rescheduled," she said, and handed him back his phone. "Thanks."

"No problem. Uh, can I drop you off somewhere?" He gathered up his presentation materials.

"Thanks. I have my car." She hesitated, wishing she could draw out the moment a little while longer.

"Then I'll see you on Monday."

"Two o'clock. Any problems, give me a call."

"Sure."

They walked out together.

"My car is right across the street," Stephanie said, pointing to her BMW.

"Nice ride."

She grinned up at him. "Thanks. A treat to myself for my last big account."

"Must have been some account."

"Maybe I'll tell you about it one day," she said, and smiled.

"Love to hear that story."

"See you Monday," she said, and sauntered across the street.

What in heaven's name was wrong with her? She put the car in gear, checked her mirrors and pulled off. She was flirting with an obviously married man. Maybe it was some kind of defect in her personality, some masochistic gene that reared its ugly head whenever a married man entered her sphere. Not again, never again. No matter how sexy, handsome, rich, famous or intelligent. No more married men. Period.

She repeated the mantra all the way to her next appointment, but all during the meeting with Sylvia, she couldn't keep Anthony "Tony" Dixon off her mind.

This was not good.

When she arrived at the facility, the staff was preparing the residents—they preferred the term *residents* as opposed to patients—for dinner.

"Ms. Moore," the head nurse greeted her. "You'll be joining Samantha for dinner?"

"Yes. How is she today?"

The nurse smiled. "She had a very good day today. She actually seemed happy."

"Thanks. I'll go see her now."

Stephanie walked down the pristine hallway to

her sister's room. She knocked lightly on the door and walked in.

Samantha was sitting in a chair by the window.

"Hey, sweetie." Stephanie slowly approached. "How are you today?" She stroked Samantha's hair and knelt down in front of her. "It's me, Steph." She lifted Samantha's chin with the tip of her finger so that their eyes met. Stephanie smiled and for an instant a brief light of recognition seemed to shine in Samantha's eyes. But like morning mist it disappeared.

Stephanie pulled up a chair and sat in front of Samantha. "I want to talk to you about some things. So much has been going on." She held her sister's hands as she told her all about her job, the mistakes she'd made with Conrad, the opportunity that was opening up for her with the spa, and starting her own business. She laughed, she talked and she cried, unburdening her soul, needing to get it all out to someone who wouldn't judge her, wouldn't think less of her. She rested her head on her sister's lap and something she only dreamed about happened.

She felt her sister's hand on her hair, patting her head the way she used to when they were little girls. The moment was so precious, so fragile, so surreal she dared not move.

Stephanie slowly reached up and took Samantha's hand and held it. She lifted her head and looked into Sam's eyes, hoping against hope that she would see something behind those vacant brown eyes. And for the first time in more than a decade she did. Herself. And then the moment was gone.

"Sam, Sam, come back to me," she pleaded. "Please." She clasped Samantha's cheeks in her palms. But Samantha had retreated to that place that Stephanie could not reach.

When Stephanie returned home she was ready to call it a night, even though it was only eight o'clock. After the visit with Samantha she was mentally and emotionally exhausted.

She hung up her jacket and took her cell phone out of her bag to put it on the charger and was surprised to see that a message was waiting for her. Must have come in while she had it turned off at the facility.

She dialed in for her message. And the last person she needed to hear from was on the other end. Anthony Dixon.

"It was great meeting you and I'm really happy that you selected me to work on your project. I know this may seem out of line, but I'd rather ask on the phone than in person and get shot down. I was hoping that on Monday after our meeting at the house I could take you out, maybe for a drink or to listen to some music in the Village. Anyway, you have a few days to think it over. Have a great evening and I'll see you on Monday."

She played the message again just to make sure

she'd heard him right. She blew out a breath and pressed the off button on her phone.

She'd heard him right. Damn, damn, damn.

Chapter 38

Ann Marie was working on the paperwork to get Stephanie's PR business incorporated. She'd settled on using her name for her corporation, which made things pretty easy. Ann Marie had done a name search and it was clear. The whole process would take a few weeks, but in the meantime she'd gotten Stephanie set up with a doing-business-as certificate until her official paperwork came through.

Funny how things work out, she thought as she sealed the forms in the envelope, ready to be mailed. She and Stephanie, for reasons that escaped them both, had never really gotten along. Their very strong personalities always clashed. So for them to have found a way to bridge the divide was a major accomplishment. She supposed she owed some of that to her budding relationship with Raquel. Having Raquel back in her life had changed her, forced her to examine her past, her present and her motives for living her life the way she had. She knew deep in her heart that she still had a long way to go to heal the wounds of her youth, but even small steps can eventually get you to where you want to go.

They were scheduled to meet later that evening at Barbara's place to go over the details and bring each other up to speed on what had been accomplished so far. She put all her notes together and slipped them into her briefcase to take with her. She had a closing that morning on a commercial property in Queens and wouldn't be back in the office. As a matter of fact, she needed to hurry. The president was in town for a meeting at the U.N. and she knew traffic in Manhattan would be horrific.

She was just getting ready to leave when the office secretary knocked on her door.

"These just arrived."

Ann Marie couldn't see the secretary's face for the profusion of flowers that she held in her hands. She jumped up from her seat and helped set the flowers on her desk.

"Where in the world did these come from?" she asked while searching for a card.

"FTD dropped them off and I signed for them. That's all I know. But someone thinks you're really special." She turned and walked out.

Ann Marie stood with her hands on her hips, surveying the riot of color. There had to be at least three dozen roses in all of their colors resting in the most exquisite crystal vase. She gently moved the blooms around, hunting for the card. She found it tucked down inside.

Excited, she pulled the card out of the tiny envelope.

"I miss you desperately. Terrance."

She stumbled back. Her hands shook. Terrance? What kind of bloody trick was this? She read the card again. Yep, that's what it said. But it couldn't be right. Terrance had no idea where she was and that's the way she wanted to keep it.

Her heart raced and his devilishly handsome face sprung before her eyes. Her mind ran in a million directions at once. She couldn't get her thoughts together. She spewed a string of cusswords before darting out to the front office.

"Carol, you said you signed for the flowers."

"Yes?" She frowned in confusion. "Is something wrong?"

"Where did you say they came from?"

She shrugged for a moment. "FTD, those flower-delivery people."

Ann Marie's eyes darted around the room, searching for someplace to land. She bit down on her newly manicured nail. "Can you get me the 800 number? No, never mind, I'll do it myself." She ran back to her cubicle, forced herself to sit down and concentrate on the numbers on the phone. After several tries she got the operator who connected her to FTD headquarters.

She listened to elevator music for a good five minutes and knew she was going to scream if someone didn't talk to her and soon. Finally, a too-cheery sales rep got on the phone.

Ann Marie talked so fast, her accent so thick, the rep had to stop her and beg her to start over. Ann Marie drew in a long calming breath. She shut her eyes for an instant and started again.

"I just received a delivery. I need to know who sent it and from where. Can you do that?"

"I'll do the best I can, ma'am." She asked Ann Marie a couple of questions and then put her on hold.

Ann Marie held the phone in a death grip as she paced the tiny confines of her space.

"Ma'am?"

"Yes!"

"The order was placed by a Terrance Bishop."

She felt faint. "Can you tell where it was sent from?"

"I'm sorry, ma'am, I can't. It was done online. Is there anything else I can help you with today?"

"No…thank you."

"Enjoy your flowers, ma'am, and thank you for using FTD."

Ann Marie plopped down in her seat and stared at nothing. How did he find her? Better still, why had he looked? What did he want? *I miss you desperately.*

Her temples pounded. She hadn't seen him in more than twenty years. He was a part of her past that she dare not revisit.

Her intercom buzzed and she leaped an inch in the air.

"Yes?"

"You're going to be late for the closing."

Ann Marie swallowed hard. "Thanks. I'm leaving now."

She shook her head to clear it, gathered her things and left the office. When she stepped outside she surveyed the street like a CIA operative. Was he out there? Was he watching? Was he going to walk up behind her and whisper something naughty in her ear and all would be lost—again?

She circled the block three times before she finally found her car, right where she'd parked it. Get a grip. You're really losing it. She took a minute to collect herself once she was behind the wheel, but all the way from Manhattan to Queens she kept seeing Terrance's grinning face in every man she encountered.

The closing was a complete blur, as was the rest of her day. By the time she arrived at Barbara's house she was a basket case.

"What in the world is wrong with you?" Barbara asked when Ann Marie came through the door.

She had a vacant look in her eyes, she'd chewed off all her lipstick and her hands were visibly shaking.

"Nothing." She walked past Barbara and into the living room where she immediately took a fresh bottle of Courvoisier out of her purse and poured a two-finger drink.

Barbara shut the door and followed Ann Marie inside. The last time she'd looked so out of sorts it was because Raquel had turned up on her doorstep. But that time, Ann Marie was more "vexed," as she would have put it, this time she looked almost terrified.

"Did something happen?" Barbara asked tentatively.

Ann Marie looked up at her. "I got flowers today."

"That's a good thing. Isn't it?" Her lips curled in a semblance of a smile.

"No, mon, it ain't no good t'ing."

"Oh." She sat down.

Ann Marie placed her bottle of brandy on the table. "They from Terrance."

"Who?"

"Terrance, chile. Terrance Bishop, Raquel's pop."

Barbara's neck jerked back. "Oh." She thought he was dead or worse. Guess not.

The doorbell rang.

"Be right back."

Ann Marie grabbed Barbara by the wrist. "Don't say nutin' to dem, hear."

"Uh, sure. No problem." She went to the door. It was Stephanie and Elizabeth.

"Come on in." Then in a hush, "Don't mention anything to Ann Marie about…anything."

They grimaced. "What?" they chimed off-key.

"Just come in and don't say anything," she said, barely moving her lips.

Stephanie huffed and walked in. Elizabeth shot Barbara a curious look and followed Stephanie inside.

Following Barbara's cryptic instructions, Elizabeth and Stephanie sat down and didn't say a word, not even hello, thinking that simple salutation might be off limits, too.

Ann Marie looked from one to the other then shot Barbara a death stare.

"She told ya, didn't she?"

They shook their heads, not daring to speak.

"I swear, I didn't say a word." Barbara crossed her heart.

Ann Marie poured herself another drink. "Well, if ya must know…"

In a series of halting sentences, Ann Marie told them all about Terrance Bishop, how she came to meet him, love him and leave him. And now, somehow he'd found her.

"Maybe it's a good thing," Elizabeth offered.

Ann Marie shook her head. "If ever there was a man no good for a woman it's 'im."

"But why, Ann?" Barbara asked. "You said you

loved him, and if he can upset you this much so many years after the fact, maybe you still do."

She lowered her head, resting her arms on her thighs. "He the only man that can make me lose myself, lose my control over my feelings. When I'm with him I don't know who I am anymore. He consumes me."

Stephanie, of all people, slid next to Ann Marie on the couch and put her arm around her shoulders. "But you're not sixteen anymore, Ann, you're a big woman, as you would say. If he does come back, you can handle him."

She looked up at Stephanie, doubt wavering in her eyes. "Ya t'ink?"

"Yeah, me t'ink." She grinned and Ann Marie smiled for the first time all night.

"You're right, I'm a big woman now. Not some innocent t'ing he can do what he want wit'."

"Exactly!" Elizabeth said.

Barbara breathed in relief. It was a tough job being the bearer of secrets, so she figured she might as well unburden herself, too.

She stood up. "Now that we have that out of the way…"

Chapter 39

"Oh…my goodness," Elizabeth said.

Stephanie stood up to get a better look. "Is it real?"

"Chile, me no care if you keep the man or not, keep the damn ring," Ann Marie said.

Barbara slipped the ring on her finger and showed it off. "It is something, isn't it?"

"What are you going to do, are you going to marry him?" Elizabeth asked.

Barbara pursed her lips. "I've been thinking it over. Hard. I don't know."

Ann Marie waved her hand. "Like I said, keep the ring. Hard times hit and you have it made."

"It's a lot to consider," Elizabeth said. "I know you'll make the right decision."

"But that rock can sure help," Ann Marie said, and took another swallow of her drink.

Stephanie was unusually quiet.

"What do you think, Steph?" Barbara asked, hoping to draw her out from the place she'd retreated.

Stephanie focused on Barbara. "Sis, I'm the last person to ask questions regarding love and relationships. I'm sure you will do the right thing." There'd be time, she was sure, to tell them about Anthony. Tonight wasn't the night, especially since she had no idea what she was going to do.

"Well, now that we have our personal dramas out of the way, let's get down to business," Barbara said after returning from her bedroom to put the ring away.

Stephanie started first, giving them all the details about her campaign plans and target dates. Starting next week she would begin contacting the newspapers and local television stations about the grand opening and sending out invitations. The flyers and business cards would be ready to be picked up in a week and she could start soliciting for clients. The target: businesses. She tossed out the idea of running some ads on radio stations, and the women agreed. Ann Marie said she could definitely come up with a list of potential clients from her database. Elizabeth told them that she wanted to be responsible for the day-to-day operations and since she would be living on-site, it would work out perfectly. They all unanimously agreed. And she would work with Desiree and Dawne to plan the menu for the grand opening, as well as with Raquel in planning the layout and decor. Barbara brought them up to speed regarding the purchase of the equipment and asked Stephanie, the techie of the bunch, to check into getting at least three computers. She added that to her list of tasks.

By the time they'd finished hashing out the details and setting a timeline it was nearly midnight and they hadn't eaten, something that had never happened before. Barbara offered to order pizza from Dominos, but the ladies declined, needing sleep more than food.

Barbara said her good-nights and prepared for bed. Things were really coming together, she mused as she got undressed. In a matter of weeks, the plan that sounded so outrageous only months earlier would be realized.

Just as she slid under the covers the phone rang and her life took yet another turn.

The baby wasn't his.

She lay awake for the better part of the night repeating over and over his words. "The baby isn't mine." She had a proposal, a ring and no baby mama drama. He said he'd be back to New York in time for their grand opening. He wished that he could come back sooner but he couldn't, as the team would be on the road. They would talk when he got into town. Remember that I love you, he'd said before hanging up.

She reached over to her nightstand and picked up

the velvet box. She opened it and stared at her possible future.

What was she going to do now?

The next few weeks were a whirlwind of activity.

The construction crew put the finishing touches on the house and Raquel oversaw the delivery of the furniture—everything from curtains and towels to couches, equipment and kitchen supplies. Dawne and Desiree had special menus printed up and worked on preparing the dinner for the grand opening, scheduled for September first.

As promised, Stephanie secured radio spots on two major stations in New York, and the all-news channel New York 1 had agreed to cover the grand opening. She successfully managed to sidestep Tony's offers of breakfast, lunch or dinner, sticking to her mantra to stay away from married men.

Ann Marie compiled an impressive guest list of who's who and Stephanie added to it from her treasured Rolodex. Barring a natural disaster, the opening would be the major hit of the season.

Elizabeth, with a lot of help from Ron, moved into her new digs on the top floor and ran the comings and goings of the setup like a seasoned captain. With her divorce finalized, she had no qualms about inviting Mr. Powers up for a nightcap at the end of the day.

Barbara secured the services of two interns from the Swiss Institute who would offer complimentary massages during the opening. If they worked out and they acquired the number of clients they anticipated, she planned to hire them on a full-time basis.

Now all that was left to do was wait on the big day.

Chapter 40

"I've never been so nervous in my life," Barbara said as she paced the gleaming parquet floors. She peeked out the window for the umpteenth time, praying that the weather would hold up and not give in to the deluge that the forecasters had predicted.

"I know what you mean," Elizabeth said, wringing her hands. "How do I look?"

Barbara turned away from the window. "Beautiful," she said, her smile reaching her eyes. "You wear love well."

Elizabeth walked up to Barbara and took her hands. "And what about you?"

Barbara drew in a breath. "I've made my decision, and if Michael shows up tonight I—"

"They're here!" Ann Marie shouted. "The news van just arrived. And cars are pulling up out front!" Her three-inch heels beat out a rapid path to the front door.

Stephanie, looking model beautiful, came running

out from the back room, her newly done weave bouncing and behaving on her bare shoulders.

Barbara and Elizabeth looked at each other, their expressions beaming with anticipation.

"This is it, girl," Barbara said.

"Let's do it."

During the next two hours the house was filled with men of every ilk: short, tall, dark, light, young, old, in shape and out. It was a boutique that every red-blooded woman could only fantasize about—men, men, men! The pure male scent and essence of them filled the rooms as they freely roamed about, getting the grand tour. It may have been raining water outside but it was raining men inside of Pause.

Desiree and Dawne were the perfect hostesses, ensuring that their special guests were adequately fed. Raquel pointed out the benefits of the contemporary but ergonomic furnishings that helped to not only relax the mind but the body, all set against the historical structure of the building.

"This is incredible," Ron whispered in Elizabeth's ear when he was finally able to steal a minute with her.

"I can hardly believe this is really happening." She stepped close to him and pressed her palm against his hard chest. She was finally ready to take the leap. "Let's celebrate, later…at my place."

He smiled. "Say no more."

Upstairs, Stephanie was in deep conversation with a potential client when she felt a presence behind her. She turned to see Anthony watching her. She wrapped up her talk and gracefully excused herself.

"Well, hello. I wasn't sure if you would make it."

"I wouldn't miss it." He looked around. This is really something. You all should be proud."

"We are. The artwork and photos that you did were a major help." She drew in a breath to keep herself in check. "I really should get back to the guests. Thanks for coming. Enjoy yourself." She made a move to leave.

"Steph, wait."

Her heart pounded. "Yes?"

"I think there's something that you should know about me…. I'm not married."

Barbara tried to concentrate on the conversation between two gentlemen who'd just signed up for Pause, but her eyes kept drifting to the door. Michael had yet to arrive. Maybe it was a sign, maybe it was just as well. Then why did she feel so let down?

Out of the corner of her eye she caught a flurry of activity and flashbulbs began going off in rapid succession. He stood head and shoulders above everyone else and she suddenly felt like a young girl whose prince had just rode in on a white horse. Her heart was racing so hard and fast that she felt light-headed.

"Go rescue your man," Ann Marie whispered in her ear.

But she couldn't seem to move and she didn't have to. He was walking her way. And like the Red Sea, everyone parted to give him space, following him with their eyes and with their cameras.

He looked down into her upturned face with a love so strong burning from his eyes that she thought she'd cry from the pure beauty of it.

"I told you I'd make it," he said only to her.

Ann Marie felt a tap on her shoulder. She turned.

"Mama, you have a phone call."

"A call? Did they say who it was?"

"I could barely hear them over all the noise."

"Thanks, sweetie, I'll take it in the back office." She excused herself and went to the office and closed the door.

A red light was flashing on the multilined phone. She pressed the button.

"Hello, this is Ann Marie." She pressed a finger to her free ear to drown out the last of the noise.

"Annie, it's Terrance. I'm coming to New York and I want to see you…and Raquel."

Chapter 41

"Well, ladies, I think we did it," Barbara said as they all sat exhausted in the lounge area of Pause.

The last of the guests had finally departed and Desiree, Dawne and Raquel volunteered to clean up. Close to one hundred men had signed up on the spot, paying with cash and credit card for exclusive membership. They were on their way, and with all the publicity the spa would get they were on the map, as well. They had clients that would be coming from as far away as Washington, D.C. The sky was the limit.

"I think you're right," Elizabeth said, laughter lifting her voice.

"We need to get good and drunk more often. No telling what we could come up with next," Stephanie quipped.

"I could sure use one," Ann Marie said. She looked from one to the other. "Terrance called. He wants to see me."

"And?" they said in unison.

"And…I'm a big woman now after all, right? It's time that Raquel met her pop."

"Absolutely!"

"Go for it, Annie," Stephanie said. "How often do we get second chances?"

"Yes, Annie, take it from me. It's always better the second time around," Elizabeth said, her mind already envisioning her night with Ron christening her bed.

"I'm going to take a chance, too," Stephanie announced. "With Tony." She told them about how she'd stuck to her guns when she believed he was married and how he'd told her tonight that he had been, nearly five years earlier. After he lost his wife he'd never taken off his ring. He saw no reason to until now.

"Steph, I'm so happy for you. Just take your time, okay?" Ann Marie said.

"I will." She hesitated a moment then looked at her friends. "And I want all of you to meet my sister…soon."

They were all silent for a moment, understanding the importance of Stephanie's trust in them.

"I have an announcement to make," Barbara said, standing up, breaking the poignant silence.

The trio looked at her in anticipation. She held out her left hand and the diamond snapped, crackled and popped in the light.

A collective gasp filled the room an instant before they swarmed around her for a group hug. Everyone began talking at once, making plans for her wedding, what they were going to wear, what roles they would play, who to invite.

All Barbara could do was laugh, her joy so complete she had no words. What more could a woman want? She had what was sure to be a thriving business, a handsome young man who adored her, and she had her friends.

There were definitely some rocky roads ahead for all of them. The paths they'd each chosen were uncertain: she and Michael, Ann and Terrance, Elizabeth and Ron, and Steph and Tony. But one thing they could always count on was each other.

"Hey, do you think we'll ever make this place coed?" Elizabeth asked as they prepared to leave.

They all looked at each other.

"Naw!"

Their laughter mixed perfectly with an unpredictable and exciting future.

Leila Owens didn't know
how to love herself let alone
an abandoned baby
but Garret Grayson knew
how to love them both.

She's My Baby

Adrianne Byrd

(Kimani Romance #10)

Silhouette®
Desire®

**Introducing an exciting appearance
by legendary
New York Times bestselling author**

DIANA PALMER

HEARTBREAKER

He's the ultimate bachelor...
but he may have just met
the one woman to change his ways!

Join the drama in the story of a confirmed
bachelor, an amnesiac beauty and their
unexpected passionate romance.

**"Diana Palmer is a mesmerizing storyteller
who captures the essence of what
a romance should be."—*Affaire de Coeur***

**Heartbreaker *is available from Silhouette Desire*
in September 2006.**

Introducing...

nocturne

a spine-tingling new line
from Silhouette Books.

These paranormal romances will
seduce you with dark, passionate tales
that stretch the boundaries of conflict,
desire, and life and death, weaving
a tapestry of sensual thrills and chills!

Don't miss the first book...

UNFORGIVEN

by *USA TODAY* bestselling author

LINDSAY McKENNA

*Launching October 2006,
wherever books are sold.*

Page-turning drama...

Exotic, glamorous locations...

Intense emotion and passionate seduction...

Sheikhs, princes and billionaire tycoons...

This summer, may we suggest:

THE SHEIKH'S DISOBEDIENT BRIDE
by Jane Porter

On sale June.

AT THE GREEK TYCOON'S BIDDING
by Cathy Williams

On sale July.

THE ITALIAN MILLIONAIRE'S VIRGIN WIFE

On sale August.

With new titles to choose from every month,
discover a world of romance in our books written
by internationally bestselling authors.

HARLEQUIN *Presents*

It's the ultimate in quality romance!

Available wherever Harlequin books are sold.

www.eHarlequin.com   HPGEN06